SILENCING THE REVOLTING

"Ki!" Jessie called. "Corbett's drawn his pistol! If he shoots one of these people it's sure to start a riot!"

Ki's response was instantaneous. As he jumped and levered himself upward he somehow managed to take a *shuriken* out of his pocket. In the few seconds required for Ki to extract the blade, Corbett was bringing up his revolver.

While Corbett was still leveling his Colt, Ki's wickedly sharp throwing blade was flashing through the air. In spite of Ki's precarious position, his aim was as accurate as always. The star-pointed blade with its razor-edged cutting tips sliced into the bared wrist of Corbett's raised gun hand . . .

LONE STAR
AND THE GHOST DANCERS

★

Chapter 1

"Look ahead there, Ki!" Jessie exclaimed, pointing at the rolling prairie in front of them. "Unless I'm very badly mistaken, those men are driving off Circle Star steers!"

Ki turned his head in the direction she was indicating, but the glistening sheen formed by a skittering shower of raindrops sweeping across the prairie ahead distorted the vista of rangeland which stretched in hillocky rises and small, shallow, thickly grassed vales.

By swiveling and leaning from side to side in his saddle, Ki finally got a clear view of where Jessie had first pointed. A scant half-mile ahead, outlined against the lowering grey rain clouds, several riders were driving a small herd of cattle up the long grassed slope. Though the distance was not great, the rain blurred the usually clear air of Southwest Texas, and both cattle and riders were visible only as vague shapes through the light, steady drizzle that was advancing ahead of the real rain.

"You're right," Ki replied after blinking to help his almond eyes adjust to the new conditions. He turned back to face Jessie as he went on, "Rustlers. They've left the Circle Star alone for quite a while, and that's probably some small gang moving from a place where they're wanted by the law."

"That's what I've been thinking too," Jessie agreed. "Just a bunch of passing rustlers. It's been a while since we've been bothered by cattle thieves."

Ki nodded and said, "It's likely they spotted that little bunch of steers and decided to grab them while they had a chance."

While they'd been talking, the little sprinkling shower which was the forerunner of the big one to come had eased and was now dying. Jessie and Ki had ignored the blowing raindrops, keeping their eyes on the progress of the cattle herd as well as the riders. There were six of them, one riding as lead a bit ahead of the herd, two as point men at each side of the lead-line steers, two as backups at the rear, the last as killpecker guard, zigzagging at the rear to chouse an occasional straggling steer back into the herd.

"Rustlers or not, they know how to drive cattle," Jessie said thoughtfully. She and Ki reined their horses to a bit slower pace in order to study the cattle and the men driving them.

"They've got to know it," Ki replied. "And that means we've got to plan pretty well, Jessie."

"Yes," she nodded. "And take them by surprise. But it looks like we might have some help from the weather, Ki. Look ahead of the herd."

Ki nodded as he glanced up at the dark clouds to which Jessie was pointing. The big rainstorm that by now had advanced above the prairie had kept moving

2

rapidly in the strip of sky and was now much closer than it had been when they first saw it. The edge of the oncoming shower was only a short distance ahead of the rustlers.

Being accustomed to the random weather that visited the vast Circle Star Ranch at this time of the year, neither Jessie nor Ki had given the small warning sprinkle a great deal of thought. Such showers were commonplace in the brief period between summer and autumn; they blew in, sprinkling raindrops for a few minutes, and were pushed out of the way by the bigger rainstorm that almost always followed.

"If the real rain hits by the time we're ready to move, it'll help, all right," he agreed.

"It looks like there are only five rustlers," Jessie went on. "I might've missed seeing one, though."

"I thought I saw six," Ki replied. "But I couldn't be sure during the few minutes before the rain started."

"That's not too important. We're going after them, regardless of how many there are," Jessie told him. "I'm certainly glad that we didn't turn back when the rain clouds started blowing in. And it was lucky that I caught a glimpse of those rustlers. And that's what they must be, because we're sure that none of our hands are on this part of the Circle Star range."

"Oh, they're rustlers, all right," Ki agreed. "And those steers have got to be Circle Star cattle, even if we can't see the brands at this distance."

"For once we've caught them red-handed, or in the act, as they say in court," Jessie said. "And they haven't seen us yet, or they'd either be turning back to put up a fight or spurring to run away."

Ki had been scanning the already familiar features of the rolling rangeland ahead. Now he said, "If I circle over to the left, where that hump is, I'll be hidden from them as soon as I get behind the rise." Ki was gesturing as he spoke. "And that ridge is long enough and high enough to hide me while I'm angling to get closer to them. If we're lucky, I might even get a little bit ahead of them."

"It ought to work," Jessie nodded. "While you're circling I'll keep on moving directly toward them. Sooner or later, one of them's sure to look back and see me. You'll know, because the minute I'm sure they've spotted us, I intend to start shooting."

"Don't worry about me," Ki told her. "I'll try to get in back of that ridge they're going up right now. The ground falls away pretty sharply on the other side of it. It'll give me cover to work from while I use my *shuriken.*"

"I remember how the land lays, and your idea's good," Jessie agreed. She was sliding her Winchester out of its saddle scabbard. "With any luck, we'll be out of sight by the time I'm close enough for them to spot me. But even if that rain coming toward us gets really heavy, you'll be able to see me until I top that long rise and drop behind it."

Jessie and Ki had not stopped while they talked, but they'd reined their mounts to a somewhat slower pace than they'd been maintaining before catching sight of the rustlers. The rider in the lead of the moving cattle was standing up in his stirrups now, gesturing toward his companions, and the steers in the front of the herd were beginning to drop out of sight behind the downslope which lay beyond the long rise of the ridge.

"That man in front—the leader, I suppose—is sure to see us when he swings around this way," Jessie said.

4

"We've been lucky so far, but luck's not enough. Let's close as much of the distance as—"

She broke off and brought up her rifle as the leader turned in their direction. It was obvious that he'd be able to start shooting before she and Ki could spur to the scant cover offered by the highest of the ridge's serrated humps. Bending forward in his saddle, Ki thunked his heels on the belly of his horse and the well-trained animal responded with an instant spurt of speed.

Jessie shouldered her Winchester now and got the boss rustler in her sights. She was tightening her trigger finger at almost the same moment that the man turned in his saddle and spotted her. In the instant before Jessie could trigger off her shot, he leaned forward to grab his rifle and jerk it free. The bullet from Jessie's rifle cut the air above him and whistled harmlessly past to bury itself in the soil of the prairie.

Jessie did not have time to pump a fresh round into her Winchester before the rustler dropped from his horse. He held on to his rifle as he rolled out of the saddle and, much quicker than Jessie thought possible, let off a shot. The slug whistled past uncomfortably close to her. Her second bullet smashed into the rustler's rifle stock and ricocheted, but its impact stunned him momentarily and knocked him down. His rifle flew from his hands as he toppled to the ground.

Now the outlaw proved himself to be a fast mover. The instant that he'd landed in a sprawl on the tall range grass, he began crawling toward the spot where his rifle had fallen. Ripples in the grass marked his path. Jessie watched the tips of the swaying ground cover long enough to be sure of the outlaw's course, and then she let off two close-spaced blind shots into

5

the area just ahead of the waving grass tips that marked his path.

Shouts were sounding now from the other rustlers. The man on the ground had stopped moving. Only the light wind rippled the grass in the area where she'd last seen him. Peer as she might, she could see no trace of him now, but the experience she had gained in many fights with the lawless told her that the rustler must have abandoned for the moment any idea of recovering his weapon.

A shot cracked from the rifle of one of the other cattle thieves, but the slug was so far off-target that neither Jessie nor Ki heard the bullet's whistle. They were a good distance ahead of the spot where the man who'd been exchanging shots with Jessie had dropped off his horse, and the stretch of rangeland between them was now too great for really accurate shooting.

Wherever Jessie or Ki looked, they saw nothing moving except the small herd of cattle and the rustlers' riderless horses. With no men now to chouse them, the steers were scattering out, most of them moving idly, a few stopping now and then to graze on some patch of grass.

"Whoever those men are, they know how to take cover," Jessie called to Ki. "But they're not as smart as they might be. If they expect to get away, they'll have to get back on their horses sooner or later."

Ki replied with a wave to indicate that he understood. Then he spurred ahead, swinging in a wide circle as he rode, for now the rustlers who'd been chousing the cattle had seen that Jessie and Ki—not a band of range hands—were their only threats. A rifle cracked, and instinctively Ki rolled out of the saddle and crouched in the tall, waving grass. Shouts were coming from the rustlers now, but he could only hear the sound of their voices—what they were saying was unintelligible.

Levering himself to his knees, Ki looked around for Jessie. She was nowhere in sight, but her riderless horse was grazing placidly fifty or sixty yards away in a little hollow, and he was sure she could not be far from her mount.

"Jessie!" he called. "Don't show yourself, those outlaws are still trying to spot us."

"I saw that when I looked a minute ago," she replied. "I'm close to my horse, and I can get a glimpse of yours."

Before Ki could reply, a shot from one of the outlaws' rifles cracked, and as he dropped flat the slug whistled above him. However, he'd gotten a glimpse of Jessie's horse several yards distant, and now her voice reached him again.

"They're not going to run," she said. "But neither are we. All we have to do is wait for them to realize they'll be able to find us close to our horses. Unless they come in shooting, I'm not going to fire at them until they're close enough for you to use your *shuriken*. They won't be expecting anything but gunfire from us—that's our ace in the hole."

"Very shrewd planning, Jessie," Ki agreed. "All that we have to do is wait, and I'll be as ready as you are when they're close enough to us."

Jessie did not reply, but Ki knew that they understood one another. He crouched, poised and ready to move when the time came to launch their counter-attack.

As the minutes ticked away it became obvious to Jessie and Ki that the outlaws were not yet ready to break cover. The riderless horses that belonged to the members of the band were scattered over the prairie, and without riders to keep them bunched the steers were beginning to scatter as well. The animals were drifting away from the herd in little clumps and heading for the patches of range grass that waved so invitingly in the gusty breezes.

Suddenly shouts rose from the outlaws. When Jessie glanced toward the area from where the cries originated, she saw the rustlers scattering. One of them still had his arm raised, pointing to her and Ki. She brought her Winchester around and picked a target, got the outlaw in her sights, and squeezed off a shot. The man who was her target broke his steps and staggered for a few more faltering paces before collapsing on the ground.

If any of his companions saw him fall, they did not go to his assistance, but kept running toward their scattered mounts. Jessie shifted the sights of her rifle from one of the running men to another, trying to pick out the leader of the gang, but she could not. Then she settled for the nearest of the gang and triggered off a quickly aimed shot at his running form.

In spite of her haste, her lead found its target. The running outlaw pitched forward and fell in a tumbling sprawl, his rifle flying from his grip as he landed on the ground and lay still. None of his companions veered from their courses to help him either. One by one they found their horses. Most of them were in their saddles, bending low over the shoulders of their horses, reins slack, guiding the animals by kicks as they began to converge on Jessie's position.

Ki saw the pattern of their moves. He broke cover and started running toward the little hump where Jessie had chosen to take cover. He fingered out two *shuriken* as he ran, holding one in his right hand ready to throw, keeping the spare blade in his left hand. The report of a rifle and the dust it raised uncomfortably close to his running feet forced Ki to change his half-formed plan.

Dropping to the ground, he began rolling away from the spot where he'd landed. He heard Jessie's rifle bark again, but the rustler who'd chosen him as a target was closer now. Drawing his feet together, Ki kicked himself erect, turning and readying the throwing blade as he rose. The outlaw who was after him raised his rifle the moment he saw Ki springing up, but Ki's *shuriken* sliced into the outlaw's neck just as the man started to squeeze off his shot.

The rustler's trigger finger closed in reflex action, but his instant of shocked hesitation had ruined his aim. Ki felt the rush of disturbed air as the slug from the rifle whizzed close to his throat, missing him by a hair's breadth. Then the outlaw slumped forward in his saddle, his arms dangling slack down the sides of his mount.

Now the outlaws were no longer as eager to press their attack as they'd been a moment earlier. Shouts filled the air. Most of the words were garbled by haste and distance, but Jessie and Ki caught a few words: " . . . get the hell outa this mess!" and " . . . run while the running's still good!"

Even without their shouted exchange of words, the remaining outlaws telegraphed their intentions by their actions. Those who'd survived were wheeling their horses and spurring the animals away from the herd to find a safe place where they would no longer be in risk of taking a bullet.

There was no order to their retreat. It became a rout, a scattered dash of beaten men to the nearest place where they would be safe. Within minutes the band had vanished from the broken, hump-marked prairie, leaving three riderless horses behind them. Jessie loosed two more quick shots of encouragement to speed them on their way, then relaxed and leaned back in her saddle and looked at Ki.

"We were lucky," she said. "Especially against the odds we faced."

"I'll have to agree," Ki nodded. "But my guess is that this bunch was just a bunch of outlaws who'd drifted together and decided to travel together as well."

"I'm sure that's how it was," Jessie agreed. "Then when we started fighting them, it got to be a case of every man for himself."

"We've got a job ahead, though," Ki pointed out. "Those steers will have to be choused into a herd again and driven—" He stopped suddenly as the thud of galloping hooves reached their ears.

"They've reorganized, Ki! They're coming back!" Jessie exclaimed. She dug a handful of shells out of her saddlebag and began refilling the Winchester's magazine.

Ki reined his horse around as he said, "I'll go find a place where I can give them some second thoughts about their plans. If we take them by surprise they'll be more apt to run again."

"No!" Jessie said quickly. She ran for her horse and called to Ki over her shoulder, "We'll go together! It's not likely they'll expect us to come out shooting."

While Jessie and Ki were hurrying to their horses, the galloping hoofbeats no longer grew louder; instead they began to fade. When they mounted, from the higher vantage point of their saddles they could see the rustlers fleeing, strung out across the prairie in a disorderly, straggling line.

"It didn't take them long to lose their stomach for a fight," Jessie said, her eyes fixed on the escaping cattle thieves. "But they've got a lead we'd find hard to overcome."

"We'd never catch up with them," Ki agreed.

"I'm sure you're right," Jessie nodded. "And I'm not really inclined to stay here any longer. It'd be dark before we could get all this cleaned up, and then that cattle herd needs to be bunched. On this part of the range there's not a line shack any closer than the main house, so let's just go back there. I'll send three or four of the hands out here tomorrow to take care of things."

"That's the best thing to do," Ki replied. "We can—"

He broke off suddenly and twisted in his saddle. Though the brush with the rustlers had been brief, the sun had dropped appreciably now, and its glow was in his eyes as he peered across the undulating prairie.

"What's wrong?" Jessie asked.

"We may have been wrong, Jessie. I'm sure I heard a horse neighing behind that rise yonder."

"You think the rustlers have circled around and are coming back?" she asked. "From the way they looked and acted when they rode off, I was sure they'd just keep going."

"So was I," Ki replied without turning to face her. "You know how sound carries out here when the wind's right. What I heard from behind that rise was a neighing horse."

"We'll know soon enough," Jessie said. Like Ki, she kept her eyes fixed on the hump that broke the level, undulating prairie just ahead of them.

Their wait was short. Before they had reached the point where the ground started to rise, the heads and shoulders of three riders broke the skyline. The sun had now dropped low, the riders were shadowed by its glow behind them. Jessie raised her Winchester and was swiveling the rifle's muzzle when Ki's warning shout reached her ears.

"No, Jessie!" he called urgently. "Don't shoot! Those aren't rustlers! They're U.S. Army officers! Look at their hats! They're cavalrymen!"

Jessie lowered the muzzle of her rifle and raised her head. Blinking in the bright sky's before-sundown glow, she finally got her first clear look at the three riders coming toward them. By this time the approaching men were clearly silhouetted against the skyline. There was no mistaking their headgear. Two of them wore the garrison caps of commissioned officers, narrow at the brim and slanting up sharply to the back. The third had on the trooper's hat with its wide straight brim and four dips in the crown.

"They must have heard the shooting and come to find out what's going on," she said. "And my guess is that those rustlers got a glimpse of them and cut a shuck getting away."

"Quite likely," Ki agreed. He frowned as he went on, "I wonder what's brought them here, Jessie. There's nothing at the Circle Star that would be of interest to them."

"There's certainly nothing I can think of," she agreed. "But I'm sure we'll find out why they're cutting across my range when they get close enough for us to talk without shouting—and we won't have very long to wait."

★

Chapter 2

Jessie and Ki had barely finished their brief conversation when one of the officers began waving at them. Jessie returned the wave. She and Ki saw the man who had been gesturing turn in his saddle and motion for the rider who'd kept his position at the rear of the leading pair.

Now the tail-rider spurred ahead of his companions and kicked his horse to a gallop as he started toward Jessie and Ki. The distance he had to cover was not great, and in a few moments he reined up in front of them. He was a young man, the one they'd identified as a cavalry trooper. He brought his hand up in a salute as his horse came to a halt and looked from Jessie to Ki with a puzzled frown for a moment. He was trying to decide whether he should talk to Jessie or to Ki, and finally settled on speaking into the vacant air between them.

"I'm Corporal Ferris, from Fort Davis," he said. "I

hope you folks don't mind, but I got orders from the officers back yonder to ask you a question or two."

"Go right ahead," Jessie nodded. "I suppose you're looking for a road? Or perhaps one of the ranches hereabout?"

"You guessed right both times, ma'am," the cavalryman replied. "But we heard some shooting, too, just a little bit ago. That's why we left the trail we was following, to see what was going on."

"I fired some of the shots you heard, and the rustlers who were trying to steal my steers fired the others," Jessie told the trooper. She swept her arm toward the steers that by now had begun grazing on the high-grassed range behind them. "As you can see, the steers are scattered and those loose horses wandering around belonged to the rustlers."

"You mean all of 'em didn't get away?"

"Jessie's a very good shot," Ki broke in to say. "If the range grass wasn't so high, you'd see a couple of bodies laying back there."

"I hadn't gotten around to mentioning that yet," Jessie said. "Not that I need to explain anything. Of course the ones who were left alive got away."

"Well, ma'am, it'd appear like to me that you sure had every right to do what you done," the soldier said.

"Oh, of course I did," Jessie agreed. "If you happen to've been brought up in this part of the country, you'll know that ranchers and rustlers don't mix together on very friendly terms."

"Even if I wasn't brought up any place close by, I've been stationed out here long enough to learn a few things," the young soldier nodded. "I know that it'd have to be sorta like it was between the army and

14

the Indians for such a long time."

"You mean shoot first and ask questions later on?" Jessie smiled.

"Something like that," he replied. After a momentary pause he went on, "It sounded like a pretty good mixup, but I guess it's all over now?"

"It is unless they come back," Jessie nodded. "Of course, we're not expecting them to do that."

"No, I don't reckon they will," the cavalryman agreed. "Now, if you can just tell me the closest way to get to the Circle Star Ranch, I'll thank you kindly and let you go about your business."

"You're on Circle Star range now," Ki told him before Jessie could reply. "This lady is Miss Jessica Starbuck, and the Circle Star is her property."

Jessie broke in to ask the cavalryman, "Do you mind telling me why you're interested in the Circle Star?"

"I was ordered by the general to inquire, ma'am," the soldier told her. "It wasn't my place to ask him any questions about why. Now, begging your pardon in advance, I've got to turn away from you while I signal the officers to come ahead."

"I don't suppose they'd object if you told me who they are?"

"One's Brigadier General Nesbitt, ma'am," the man said quickly. "The other one's Captain Bonham. The general's from back East, but Captain Bonham's stationed where I am, at Fort Davis. And you're the lady they've come here looking for. Now if you'll just excuse me for a minute, I'll signal to 'em to ride on up."

As soon as he'd finished his explanation the soldier rose in his stirrups, half-turned to face the waiting officers and gave the cavalry's full arm-wave signal to advance. It was obvious that the officers had been waiting for it. They started at once toward Jessie and Ki.

"Now that you've done your duty, suppose you answer my question," Jessie suggested as the soldier settled back into his saddle and turned toward them. "I'd like to know why the army's showing so much interest in me and the Circle Star."

"Ma'am, I'm going to have to ask you to wait a minute for an answer to that," he replied. "General Nesbitt's the one who better do the explaining. I reckon you know that when you're in the army, nobody tells us enlisted men much of anything."

"Yes, so I've heard," Jessie smiled. "But you can't have been riding with those officers from—" She stopped short and went on, "I'm sorry if I seem to be plaguing you. It's just occurred to me that Fort Davis is quite a distance from here. Whatever it was that brings you here must be something quite important for a general to travel this far."

"I can't say as to that, ma'am," the cavalryman replied. "But I got orders not to talk to nobody about what the officers says or does."

"And you said you're stationed at Fort Davis?" Jessie asked.

"I guess I did mention that, ma'am, and I don't suppose it done no harm," the soldier replied. "But like I said, all I know is, my troop's top kick told me I was to report to General Nesbitt's orderly and the orderly told me I was going on a mission with the general and captain. Then just before we started out, the general said I was to keep my mouth shut about anything I seen or heard."

"You mean this is some sort of a secret meeting?" Ki asked.

16

"With all respect, sir, I can't say.yes or no or maybe," the cavalryman replied. "And like I just told the lady here, even if I knew what all this is about I got orders not to say a word to nobody about it, on the post or off."

"We won't ask you any more questions, then," Jessie promised. "I certainly wouldn't want to get you into any sort of trouble, and I'm sure we'll learn the reason for this visit soon enough."

She broke off as the two cavalry officers reached them and reined in. Both the men saluted before doffing their caps. Even before they'd gotten close enough to speak, Jessie had identified them not only by the difference in their ages, but by the insignia on their shoulder straps: the single silver star of the general and the two silver bars of the captain.

Jessie took the initiative without delay. She said, "I'm Jessica Starbuck, General Nesbitt. Your orderly's already told me your names, and I've no idea why you're visiting me, but I'm sure that's something we'll be discussing later. Let me welcome both you and Captain Bonham to the Circle Star." Without pausing, she indicated Ki and went on, "And this is Ki, my trusted assistant and companion."

Ki did not nudge his horse up to shake hands with the officers, but followed their example and nodded to acknowledge the introduction.

"I hope we're not intruding, Miss Starbuck," the general said. "But I assure you that our reason for being here is not just a casual visit."

"I can understand that quite well," Jessie replied.

"We heard shots being fired a short time ago," Captain Bonham said. "I hope there hasn't been trouble here on your range."

"As I've just explained to your orderly, Ki and I were riding around the ranch on one of our routine inspection trips," Jessie replied. "We ran into a little bunch of cattle rustlers and swapped a few shots with them."

"So that was the shooting we heard!" Nesbitt exclaimed. "When we heard rifle shots we could tell they must be coming from somewhere close by, so I decided we'd better turn off the trail we'd been following to find out what the trouble was."

"And it was over before you got here," Jessie said.

"You two drove them off by yourselves?" the general asked. "How many rustlers were there?"

"A half-dozen," Jessie replied. "They weren't expecting to be disturbed because we're quite a distance from the Circle Star's main house. We managed to surprise them, and they didn't really put up much of a fight. There are two, perhaps three, of them dead in the tall grass back there."

"Is there anything we can do to help you, Miss Starbuck?" Nesbitt asked.

Jessie shook her head. "Thank you, General, but I'll send some of my own men out here tomorrow to bury the bodies of the two men who were killed and clear the range and gather up the cattle that might've strayed from that little herd the rustlers were trying to steal from me."

"As long as you're sure—" the general began.

Jessie held up her hand to stop him. "I'm very sure," she said. "Here on the Circle Star we take care of our own problems all the time. Now, it's getting late in the day, and it's a fairly long ride to the main house. We'd better start right away, then we won't have to ride so far in the dark."

"How much of a ride is it?" Bonham asked.

18

"Just a bit more than an hour," Jessie replied. "Probably more, if your horses are as tired as ours."

"This is our fourth day in the saddle," General Nesbitt said. "And I haven't quite gotten rested up after my trip west from Washington. An hour doesn't sound at all bad, though. If you don't have anything more to keep you here, Miss Starbuck, suppose we get started."

"Even if we've agreed to put off discussing the reason for your visit until tomorrow, after we've had a chance to rest up a bit, I'm sure you won't mind me asking you a question, General Nesbitt," Jessie said.

"Of course not," Nesbitt replied. "What is it that you want to know?"

Jessie and Ki were sitting with the two army officers in the spacious study of of the Circle Star's main house, enjoying after-dinner coffee. At Nesbitt's suggestion the young corporal had been put into the care of Ed Wright, the Circle Star foreman, to be fed supper and provided with a bunk for the night.

"You've mentioned that your visit here isn't a casual one," Jessie went on. "Now, I've been wracking my brain to think of some reason why I should be selected to help the army in any way. I have a few friends in the military service, of course, but it's always been my impression that the army's main job is fighting."

Nesbitt did not answer immediately, but sat quietly thoughtful. At last he said, "You're right about the army's job being to fight our country's battles, Miss Starbuck. But it's also our job to remove the need to fight."

For a moment Jessie frowned as she tried to interpret what the general had said. At last she asked, "I'd really appreciate knowing more right now, but I understand

19

why you're reluctant to give me an immediate explanation. Isn't it that we've just met, and you'd like to have time to think of the best way to tell me about whatever reason has brought you here?"

"You're a very discerning lady, Miss Starbuck," Nesbitt replied. "And I won't beat around any bushes. Yes, that is part of my reason for wanting to do some thinking before we sit down to talk. I hope you don't object?"

"Not in the least," Jessie assured him. "You've been traveling for some time, you need to think in private, and I can't say that I blame you. There are times when I need to do the same thing myself."

"I can see that we're going to understand one another," Nesbitt nodded as he stood up. "Now, in spite of enjoying your company since finishing that delicious dinner, I've been thinking more and more about the bed that's waiting for me in my room upstairs. I imagine your ranch hands will be getting up early?"

"They certainly will. So will I, for that matter."

"Of course," Nesbitt replied as he started for the door. "I'm an early riser myself, so if you'll excuse me I'll say good night now and be looking forward to our talk in the morning."

"Fine," Jessie replied. "I'm ready to call it a day, too, but before going to bed I need to step over to the bunkhouse and tell my foreman what needs to be done tomorrow."

Ki had gotten out of his chair when General Nesbitt stood up, and made himself inconspicuous, a part of the background. Now he said to Jessie, "If you want me to save you a bit of walking, I'll be glad to go to the bunkhouse and talk to Ed. Otherwise, I'll be off to bed too."

"Thanks, Ki, but I want to go on past the bunkhouse and look at Sun," Jessie answered. As Ki nodded and turned to go, she explained to Bonham, "Sun's my palomino saddle horse, a very special one. A stone got caught in one of his hoof clefts a day or so ago, and lamed him a bit. I'd like to see how he is."

"I don't blame you, Miss Starbuck," Bonham told her. "If I had a fine palomino, I'd sure take good care of him."

"He doesn't lack for care," Jessie smiled. "Now, let me get started."

Captain Bonham had not interrupted the conversation between Jessie and the general. Now as Nesbitt started for the stairs he said to Jessie, "Would you mind if I invited myself to go along with you, Miss Starbuck? Before I turn in, I'd like to stretch my legs after the long day we've had in the saddle."

"Why, I'd enjoy your company, Captain," Jessie replied. "Come right along."

They stepped out into the moonlit night. In addition to the glowing windows of the rambling two-story main house, lights still showed in the dining room–cook house and the small two-room cottage occupied by the ranch foreman. The bunkhouse was dark, and beyond it on the gently rising upslope the six barns that held hay, wagons, tools, stacked rolls of barbwire fencing and all the other materials required to keep the Circle Star functioning showed as massive black silhouettes against the bright, moonlit sky.

Gesturing toward the night vista, Bonham said, "Even if I've only seen your ranch headquarters in the dark, it's certainly impressive. You've got as many buildings here on your place as I've seen in some of the little towns in this part of Texas."

"I'd never thought of comparing the Circle Star to a town, but I suppose it is, at that," Jessie agreed, indicating with a wave of her hand the direction they'd be taking.

They'd crossed from the main house to the fore-man's quarters while they talked. Jessie stepped up to the door and tapped gently.

Ed Wright opened it. Upon seeing Jessie and Bonham, he asked, "You need a bunk for somebody else, Miss Jessie?"

"No, all our guests are settled in the main house, Ed," Jessie replied. "But I didn't have time before supper to tell you that there's a cleanup job on the southeast forty, where Ki and I had that brush with the rustlers."

"I've been wondering about that myself," Wright nodded. "I was going to ask you in the morning, but it'll be better if I know tonight."

"I'm sure those men who were trying to steal our cattle cut some fences," Jessie went on. "And there are at least two bodies in the grass. I think you can just bury them in some corner where the graves won't be trampled. You can mark them or not, that's up to you. The only other thing on my mind is that some of our steers are sure to've found that fence gap and straggled off our range."

"That's just what I needed to know, Miss Jessie," Wright told her. "Thanks a lot. I'll see to all of it."

"Good," Jessie said. "Now, Captain Bonham and I are going up to visit Sun. Have you had a chance to look at him today?"

"No, ma'am, but Chonky did," Wright replied. "He says it'll be three or four days more before that hoof's ready to get another shoe put on."

"Well, I'll be glad when I can ride Sun again," Jessie said. "Now we'll stop interrupting you and be on our way."

As Jessie and Bonham started down the gentle slope leading to the Circle Star's outbuildings, the officer said, "I'll say it again: I don't think I've ever been on a ranch this size before, Miss Starbuck. I know there's a lot of big ones in Texas, but this one really takes the cake."

"I can't take any credit for it," Jessie replied. "It was my father who put the Circle Star together. He needed a place where he could be alone for a while from time to time, away from the bustle and stress of the businesses he had to look after. He was—" She stopped short.

Bonham waited a moment, then went on, "I see. I guess . . ."

Then he fell silent, realizing belatedly from the changed tones of Jessie's voice that he might be starting to tread on uncertain, perhaps unhappy, ground. His instinct was sound, for as was so often the case when her father's name was mentioned, thoughts of the father she'd adored so deeply had begun flashing through Jessie's mind.

She remembered the great energy Alex Starbuck possessed and how she had admired him for all the things that he accomplished in his life. Jessie knew that as she got older her respect for him grew even more, if that were possible. The extensiveness of his holdings and the diversity of the business that he had conceived of, and prospered with, were mind-boggling.

Then Jessie realized that while she was lost in thought, Captain Bonham was standing and looking uncomfortable, probably regretting that he had brought about this change in mood.

She explained, "My father's death was a great shock and outrage to me. This ranch that you've expressed so much admiration for isn't even the biggest of his many enterprises. As you may imagine, I loved him very much."

Bonham replied, "It must be very difficult to live all alone here with the painful memory of your father's death."

Jessie said, "I don't feel all alone. Ki's position as my most trusted advisor has kept me from being alone. Ki's first loyalty was to my father, and upon my father's death, Ki's loyalty was transferred to me. Ki knew much about my father's businesses and all about his philosophy. Many times we have found ourselves carrying on my father's legacy in not only his management of his businesses but also in fighting evil in the West or wherever it finds us."

Bonham said, "You are a very unusual woman, Jessica Starbuck. Most women don't talk of managing businesses or fighting evil."

Jessie smiled as she replied, "My father was an unusual man, and I must take after him. His leaving me the Circle Star has been a great comfort to me. His spirit is so strong here that it helps me to do things I would never have otherwise believed I was capable of. For instance, my instincts in business are much better than women are given credit for having. I believe that I will not discredit my father's legacy in that."

Bonham smiled. "Your reputation for being capable is spreading, Miss Starbuck. You must realize that is one of the reasons that the general and I are here."

"And what are those reasons?"

"I'm not at liberty to discuss that with you," Bonham replied stiffly. "It is General Nesbitt's express wish that he present the problem to you himself."

Jessie smiled and said, "That's okay. You must understand that I am very curious about your visit. But I'll try to keep that curiosity in check until tomorrow. Anyway, here we are."

They had reached Sun's temporary enclosure. With a snorting neigh and a tossing of his head that set his long mane into a rippling that was visible even in the darkness, Sun came up to the paddock fence to greet them.

★

Chapter 3

"Good horse, Sun!" Jessie exclaimed as she stood on her tiptoes to reach across the fence and pat the palomino's head and stroke his muzzle. "You won't have to stay in here much longer. Then when you come out we'll spend a whole day just rambling around the ranch and giving you the exercise you need."

"I have an idea that you and your favorite horse get along very well together," Bonham said as he stepped closer to get a better look at Sun. "I don't even have to see this fellow in the daylight to realize that he's a very fine animal."

"Sun's so biddable that he surprises me sometimes, even after all the years I've had him," Jessie told her companion. "It's not only that he's the last gift my father gave me. From the very first time I saw Sun we seemed to have some kind of special bond between us."

"I had that feeling with a horse once, Miss Starbuck,"

the officer nodded. "It was when I was about fourteen, and doing the same day's work as a man. And I learned a real important lesson from him."

Jessie's intuition told her that the officer felt a need to share his youthful experience with someone. She asked, "What sort of lesson?"

"That horse I set so much store by broke a leg one day when I'd ridden him out to go hunting," Bonham replied. He hesitated for a moment before going on. "I was four or five miles away from home and there wasn't a thing I could do to help him. I knew I had to shoot him, so I did."

"What a terrible thing for a young man to go through!" Jessie exclaimed. "I can understand why you don't like to talk about it."

"Well, that's not quite all of what happened," Bonham went on. "And I might not admit this to anybody but an understanding lady like you, Miss Starbuck, but even if I was supposed to be a full-grown man by that time, I cried like a baby while I was carrying my saddle home."

"Oh, I can understand that," Jessie assured him. "And isn't the lesson you said you learned that life sometimes treats people unfairly?"

"That's about right," he admitted. "I guess in one way it's done me an awful lot of good to know that, but I'd a heap rather have had my horse back than to've learned that lesson. It made me sorta shy for a long time. Maybe it's one reason why I never did get married, because I was too scared of losing somebody that I put a lot of store in."

While they talked, Jessie stroked Sun's muzzle. When Bonham reached up to stroke it too, their hands brushed together. Bonham drew his hand away quickly, and

28

Jessie continued to pat and stroke Sun's head for a few moments. It was obvious that the big palomino was enjoying her touches, for Sun whinnied repeatedly as he stretched his neck and turned his head from side to side while her hands moved.

Jessie kept up her attentions for several minutes before she lowered her arms. Turning toward Bonham, she said, "I think it's time for us to be getting back to the main house."

"I can't argue about that," he nodded. "It must be around ten o'clock by now, maybe even a little bit later."

"Something like that," Jessie agreed as they turned away from Sun's enclosure and started toward the lighted windows of the Circle Star's main house. "But I'm sure that Ki has already arranged for a late breakfast, so we won't have to hurry around getting ready in the morning."

"I guess he'll knock at the door to rouse the general and me?" Bonham asked.

"Oh, of course. If he doesn't, I will. I'll admit that I'm a little bit impatient to find out about General Nesbitt's reason for coming here. From the very few remarks that he made while we were talking after supper, I've gotten the feeling that he's going to ask me to take on some sort of chore that the army wants done by someone who hasn't any connection with the service."

Bonham was quick to reply. He said, "I can't answer you as to that, Miss Starbuck. The general's been mighty close-mouthed the whole time we've been traveling together. He hasn't said a word to me about why we were coming here."

"I can understand that," Jessie said. "One thing that

my father impressed on me when I was growing up is that a secret shared is a secret lost."

"Well, that's Gospel truth," Bonham agreed. "And it's real hard for folks to learn it sometimes."

During their conversation they'd been walking steadily through the darkness toward the Circle Star's main house. They reached the point where the light came from its windows. Jessie glanced at Bonham just as he turned to look at her. Their eyes met, but no words passed between them until they were inside.

"I'm sure you remember where your room is," Jessie said. "And I always like to take a final look around the house before I go to bed, just to make sure everything's in good order. Not that we have anything to worry about, but sometimes I find a lamp that Ki or I didn't blow out, some trifling little thing such as that."

"You and him are real good friends, aren't you? Been together a long time, I'd imagine."

"As long as I can remember," she replied. "If it wasn't such a contradiction in terms, I'd say that he's been more like a mother—I never knew my mother, you see—than anything else."

"I guess I understand what you mean," Bonham, nodded. "But us standing here gabbing's just taking up time when we ought to be sleeping, so I'll bid you good night and let you take your look around so's you can get to bed too."

Jessie made her usual quick inspection of the big, rambling house and found that as usual, Ki had put everything in order after their dinner. She went up the stairway, and to her room at the end of the long corridor. As usual, the Circle Star's handyman—one of Alex's veteran hands no longer able to ride with the other hands, but capable of helping in the mess hall kitchen and doing light work—had left her room in good order.

Wasting no time as she undressed, Jessie poured water into the small stand-up tub in the alcove of her room and sponged quickly. She understood the restless feeling that at some time during her walk with Greg Bonham had suddenly invaded her mind and body after their casually accidental brushing of hands.

She'd suppressed the sudden and almost imperceptible wave their contact had given her then. Now, it was returning to her as she rubbed the drops of bathwater from her supple, compact body. The ruddy tips of her generous high-standing breasts pebbled as she rubbed and blotted them with a towel and thought of the young officer in the room just down the corridor from her own. Never one to waste time in self-debate, accustomed to making her own decisions and carrying them to completion, Jessie slipped her arms into the silk dressing gown that lay across her bed and stepped into the hall.

A faint glow from the candle in the night lamp at the foot of the stairs brightened the corridor. Jessie took the few steps needed to reach the door of Bonham's room. Not giving herself time to change her mind, she tapped on it with her fingertips.

A moment of almost inaudible rustling reached her ears from the room beyond, then the door opened. Bonham's face appeared, his neck twisting as he shielded himself behind the door. His face and one bare arm and the edge of his shoulder were visible and they glistened with tiny drops of water. The deep tanning of his face and hands formed an odd contrast with the white skin of his arms and shoulder.

"Miss Starbuck!" he said in a gasping half-whisper.

"What's wrong? There must be something that's happened to bring you here in your nightdress."

"Nothing that I know of," Jessie replied. She was very aware of his eyes moving to inspect her filmy wrap. "I'm sure that I'm not the first woman you've seen in a negligee. But this isn't the place for us to talk. Aren't you going to invite me to come in?"

"I—I'm afraid I'm not dressed to receive company," Bonham stammered. "But—" he broke off and took a half-step back as Jessie gently but firmly pushed the door open widely enough to allow her to turn sidewise and slip past him into the room.

Once inside, Jessie turned to face him. She saw then that Bonham was completely naked, and before he could move or speak she shrugged her shoulders from her dressing gown and let the garment slip to the floor.

Bonham had started to cross his hands to cover his crotch, but he forgot his intention as Jessie moved. His jaw dropped and he stared at her softly glowing nude body for a moment. Then he let his arms fall away to dangle at his sides.

"If you're thinking that I'm a lewd woman, you might be partly right," Jessie remarked. Her smile canceled the effect of her words. Keeping the tone of her voice casually conversational, she went on. "But I certainly don't knock at the door of every man who visits the Circle Star. Neither do I mind admitting that I do knock now and then at the door of a man who attracts me."

"I—I know you've certainly attracted me," Bonham admitted, his voice a bit hesitant. "But I couldn't quite bring myself to intrude on you."

"I can understand that," Jessie nodded. "And if you'd

like for me to turn around and go back to my own room, just say—"

Bonham did not give Jessie time to finish her offer. He stepped up to her and took her in his arms, then bent to find her lips with his. After a moment she felt the tip of his tongue push at her lips. She opened them and met his tongue with her own. For several moments, time stood still while they exchanged their first caresses.

Breathlessness finally forced them to part. Bonham rubbed his cheek across Jessie's shoulder as he bent down to carry his lips to her breasts. They were already budded, and he took first one tip and then the other between his lips to caress them with his tongue. Jessie pulled back her shoulders a bit to enable him to reach them more easily. Then she slid one hand down his side to his crotch and found that he was already swollen and erect.

Jessie's body was beginning to grow taut as Bonham continued stroking her soft, yielding skin and moving his lips from one budded breast to the other. She abandoned the gentle caresses that she'd been giving his erection, then brought up her hand and cradled his chin in her palm, raising his head until their eyes met.

"There's no reason to wait any longer," she whispered. "Not when there's a bed waiting for us across the room."

"I can't believe all this is happening," he told her. "I'm afraid it's a dream and if I move, I'll wake up."

"It's real enough," Jessie assured him as she lifted her head, inviting his lips.

Bonham bent to meet them with his own lips. To Jessie in her increasing eagerness, the kiss seemed to go on endlessly. While their lips were still glued together, she started moving toward the bed. Bonham did not resist her leading. They reached the bed, and only now did Jessie twist her head to break their kiss.

She fell back on the mattress, again inviting him wordlessly by spreading her thighs to be ready for him. Bonham kneeled above her and Jessie placed him quickly. He drove then, a full, deep penetration that brought an explosive gasp of delight from her.

"Wonderful!" Jessie sighed as she locked her legs around her lover's hips to hold him buried in her. She kept the pressure of her legs on him for only a few moments. Then she relaxed the firmness of her grip and whispered hoarsely, "Now *drive!*"

Bonham drove. He penetrated fully and deeply and held himself buried in Jessie's moist warmth for several moments while she twisted her hips and rolled them slowly from side to side. Now and then she sighed softly, the pleasure-sighs of being filled. Bonham did not move for a few moments, then he began to stroke slowly, with one long, deep lunge after another.

Jessie lay supine for a short while, passively accepting her lover's slowly measured stroking. When she felt the first tremors of her response beginning, she locked her legs behind Bonham's back and held him motionless, buried deep, until the anticipatory quivers of her body subsided. Then she relaxed the pressure of her legs and spread her thighs even wider. Bonham responded to her silent signal by beginning once more to drive rhythmically with increasing vigor.

Now Jessie began rising to meet his lunges instead of just accepting them. She took the position she'd been taught by the wise old geisha to whom Alex had entrusted her education in sexual matters, spreading her thighs until her upper legs were almost flat on the

34

mattress, while above her Bonham kept driving with ever more forceful thrusts.

Jessie read the silent message signaled by the increasingly short intervals of rest that he'd been allowing himself. His body began to quiver and she quelled his shudders by locking her legs again, holding him buried and motionless until his tremors subsided. Then she relaxed the tension of her thighs and released him to resume his stroking.

After a few measured lunges, Bonham began once more to step up the tempo of his driving. Jessie was almost ready, and she did not try to hold herself back any longer. Once again she began lifting her hips and rolling them from side to side as he drove. He was breathing rapidly now, and his lunges were paced faster. Jessie was also beginning to rise to the point of no return, and this time she did not try to delay its onset.

As her lover's body began to quiver she relaxed all control. Together they rose to the edge of total climax and as Bonham lunged in a final fierce thrust Jessie started quivering in the fast-mounting path to completion. They rose together, and only seconds passed by before Bonham cried out and plunged into his climactic thrust while Jessie shook and quivered through her own spasm.

Their spastic shudders rippled on and on, subsiding for brief seconds, then recurring until they faded and died and both Jessie and Bonham lay quiet and spent. Minutes ticked away before either of them moved or spoke. It was Bonham who rolled away and stretched out beside Jessie, and it was Jessie who broke the silence a few moments later.

"You're a very satisfactory lover, Greg," she said softly.

35

"You made me want to be," Bonham replied. "You're not like so many women, hanging back and making a fellow beg."

"That's not my way," Jessie agreed. "But I was taught to meet a man halfway and to give him as much pleasure as he's giving me."

"Which you certainly did. I'm not sure I could do it a second time, though, much as I'd like to."

"I don't think it'd be wise even to try," Jessie said. "Today's been a very busy one, and we'll both be equally busy tomorrow. Just a good night kiss, now, and I'll go back to my own room. Then we'll think about tomorrow night and be rested enough to enjoy it even more than we did tonight."

"I don't know when I've had a better breakfast or one I enjoyed more," General Nesbitt observed as he folded his napkin and laid it beside his cleared plate. "Your Circle Star Ranch is certainly better organized than most of the ones I've visited."

"You'll have to give Gimpy—he's our cook—credit for that," Jessie smiled. "Ki and I are too busy to look over his shoulder and make suggestions. He just gives us a list of the things he needs and one of us makes sure it's filled."

"Your mentioning Ki brings something to my mind, Miss Starbuck," Nesbitt went on. "My orders from the president are to pass on his message to you in private, but I've gathered that Ki fills a place here that's rather like the president's cabinet—you don't have any secrets from each other."

"I hadn't thought of it in those terms, but you're quite right," Jessie nodded.

"Then I'm going to stretch my orders a bit," the

general said. "Captain Bonham must be informed, in the event that something should happen to me, and I'm going to ask you to bring Ki into our confidential discussion."

"I'm really glad you decided to do that, General," Jessie told him. "Ki's my good right hand, and I like for him to be on hand when there's a matter of importance to be discussed. And of course we'll both be very interested to learn what's brought you here. Suppose we move into the study, where we'll be more comfortable, and you can tell me what this mysterious situation is all about."

When the little group had settled into the more commodious accommodations of the study which had been Alex Starbuck's domain during the last years of his life, General Nesbitt drew a bulging envelope from his pocket and placed it on the small side table beside the easy chair he'd selected. He looked at Jessie, Ki, and Bonham without opening the envelope.

"I'm not going to repeat what I've already said about the confidentiality of what I'm about to tell you," he said. "I've studied this material until I know it by heart. To sum it up into a nutshell, the president is forming a very secret group that will have an important job to do and will receive no recognition or reward for doing it. In fact, if anything should go wrong, he's prepared to deny that our government had a part in it, or even knew anything about it."

"That sounds both impressive and perplexing," Jessie frowned when Nesbitt paused for breath. "I can't imagine what the reason is."

"You will when I explain," the general replied.

When Jessie opened her mouth to carry on her questioning, Nesbitt stopped her with a gesture.

"I don't usually have a great deal of confidence in the Indian Bureau," he went on. "I've read their reports and recommendations for a number of years when I was stationed in Washington as a member of the War Department's general staff. Much of what's in those reports was outright lies, a great deal was garbage designed to make their operation look better than it really was, and some was sheer nonsense."

"Then you're asking some of us to go into the Indian Bureau and try to improve it?" Jessie asked.

"Not exactly that," he answered. "Something much more important and quite a bit riskier."

"I can't imagine what that could be," Jessie said.

"You will when I explain," Nesbitt told her. He went on quickly. "I understand you've been on several of the reservations, Miss Starbuck. Am I correct?"

"Yes, of course," she told him. "Ki and I have been on a few, in New Mexico and the Arizona Territories and in the Pacific Northwest."

"Those are all reservations of the peaceful tribes," the general reminded her. "Have you had any occasion to spend any time on the Sioux reservations? What I'm referring to now are the warrior tribes, the Oglala, the Brûle, and Miniconju and Blackfoot."

"We've passed through some of them," Jessie replied. "But the Sioux Nation is made up of warrior tribes, General Nesbitt. Their men aren't like the Hopis or the Nez Percé, who've learned to live peacefully with our white civilization. But I can't see what all this has to do—"

Nesbitt raised his hand to stop her, and when Jessie fell silent he told her, "Those of us who've had access to confidential files can understand, Miss Starbuck, but those files aren't open to the public." His voice was sober as he went on. "Let me give you just one example. The Sioux are no longer a weak, divided tribe. They've formed themselves into what they call a nation, and that's the clearest sign possible that sooner or later they'll be at war with ours. We want to keep that from happening. That is the primary reason why the president has sent me to talk with you."

★

Chapter 4

Jessie was silent for a moment, a thoughtful frown forming on her face. After a moment she said, "It's flattering to know that the president remembers me, General. But what you've said sounds more than a little bit ominous. Are you positive it's really going to happen?"

"Sooner or later, Miss Starbuck," Nesbitt said. "Unless we avert it. To do that quickly will mean changing our treatment of the tribes. If we don't, they'll find a way to come together and present a common face to us. But that's something to worry about in the future. I'd like to start with the first problem, if you haven't any objections."

"Of course I don't," she agreed. "And I'll certainly admit that I'm very curious to find out why you've come here to talk to Ki and me."

"Because now that Alan Pinkerton's dead we don't

have enough manpower on the army's active investigative roster right now," Nesbitt told her, his voice sober. "At least not enough good men to do all the work that'll be required to get to the bottom of this. The Indian Bureau's so badly managed and so corrupt that it's absolutely no use to our army's general staff as a source of information, Miss Starbuck."

"So what you're really doing now is looking for some sort of reinforcements? Enlisting civilians to—well, to put it bluntly—to spy on the Indians."

"I suppose you could call it that," he agreed. "And I'll ask you to keep my visit confidential. You aren't the only one who's being called on, Miss Starbuck. Right about now there are several other senior officers who're visiting people in positions similar to yours."

"Wouldn't it be easier just to abolish the Indian Bureau and set up a new agency that would be honest and efficient?" Jessie asked.

"That's been discussed," the general replied. "And all of us on this special presidential commission agree that it's not a practical solution. First there'd be a problem of finding the right people. Then there'd be an even bigger problem, getting the Indian tribes to accept them."

"Yes, I can see that," Jessie said thoughtfully. "That's very similar to some of the jobs we face in the business world. I suppose you've already considered retraining the present Indian agents?"

"We've considered it and given it up, along with a number of other alternatives," Nesbitt replied. "The Indian Bureau's gotten too big, too cumbersome, and—well, to be blunt—too dishonest. But replacing it man by man or abolishing it and starting a new agency just aren't practical solutions."

"Perhaps I'd understand better if you'd give me some detailed information," Jessie suggested.

"Our first big problem is that we don't have enough strength left here in the West. Most of the forts west of the Mississippi have been closed or turned over to the Indian Bureau. And if I can be blunt, that bunch of thieves in the Indian Bureau is one of the big reasons why we'll have trouble if a showdown comes."

"Dishonesty?" Jessie asked. "Workers on the reservations stealing from the Indians they're supposed to be helping?"

"Exactly," Nesbitt nodded. "And I hate to admit it to anybody, even to you and Ki. Not that I'd ever deny having said it, but because it could cast an ugly shadow over the entire government. It's a brutal fact that most of the agents in charge of the reservations are more interested in stealing than they are in seeing that the money sent them to buy food for the reservations is used for that purpose. They're taking so much that there's not enough left to keep the Indians properly fed. Hunger means unrest and unrest means trouble."

"Surely the stealing could be stopped," Jessie said.

"It's not that easy," Nesbitt replied. "Remember, there are some men in the Indian Agency headquarters in Washington who get a share of the loot."

"But you must've tried—" Jessie began, and stopped when the general held up his hand.

"We've tried just about every means possible," he said. "That includes sending soldiers in civilian clothing—spies, if you want to call them that—to watch and give us a report that we can rely on, but the Indian agents seem to sniff them out. Three of the last four military men who went out on one of these assignments have been murdered."

"No wonder you've come here to the Circle Star," Jessie observed. Her voice was very sober. "I can see now that you're on a recruiting mission."

"I suppose you'd call it that," Nesbitt agreed. "And if you're puzzled why I came here to ask you to be one of our first recruits—it was the president himself who suggested it. He also instructed me to tell you that the reason he didn't write a letter confirming what I've said is that it's impossible to keep any written White House business really secret any longer."

"Too many inquiring journalists?" Jessie smiled.

"Exactly," he said, a small sour smile forming on his face. "In addition to blabbermouth clerks and administrators. They seem to be able to flatten themselves out and hide under the carpet in the White House these days."

"Don't worry about your secrets being given away by either Ki or me," Jessie said quickly. "But now that I understand the first problem, suppose we move on to the one you hinted at a moment ago."

"It's quite a bit more complicated and a great deal more important," Nesbitt frowned. "But I doubt that you'll find many top-echelon officers who'll disagree with what I believe myself, Miss Starbuck."

"And that is?" Jessie asked, raising her eyebrows.

"Let me ask you a question or two before I answer yours," Nesbitt said. Without waiting for Jessie to comment, he went on. "I know the Starbuck enterprises are scattered out pretty well here in the West. I'd imagine that you must travel a very substantial amount of time and cover a great deal of territory in supervising them?"

"Much more than I sometimes enjoy." Jessie smiled a bit ruefully as she went on. "I'd much rather spend more of my time here on the Circle Star than I do riding trains and stagecoaches or traveling on horseback."

"And in all your traveling you must learn a great deal about our Indian tribes?"

"Yes, of course," she said. "And I've kept up the policy my father established—we hire a substantial number of Indians in some of our operations. Why do you ask?"

For a moment the general did not reply, then he said very soberly, "Because information has reached the General Staff that the Sioux tribes on the Dakota reservations are taking the lead in forming an Indian army that will begin a new war of rebellion against our government."

"General Nesbitt, are you saying that the Sioux are really going to start a war and try to fight the United States?" Jessie asked.

"I believe that in their minds they've never stopped being at war with us, Miss Starbuck," Nesbitt replied. "At headquarters in Washington we keep a log of all fights between Indians and groups of whites that are reported by our forts and western field stations. Right after Sitting Bull was arrested and kept in custody, the number of fights was going down, but now it's increasing again."

"I didn't realize it was that bad," Jessie said. "But there must be a reason of some kind. Sitting Bull hasn't been let out of prison, has he?"

"No, but the General Staff is discussing the idea of freeing him," Nesbitt replied. "In the meantime, as many as three or four skirmishes are added to the list every month. Two out of three of them involve one of the Sioux tribes."

"It's odd, General, but I haven't seen any reports of

a new rash of Indian troubles in the two newspapers we subscribe to. They're the *New York Times* and *The San Francisco Chronicle,* and certainly one or both of them should have mentioned it."

"Well, we haven't tried to hide the situation," Nesbitt said. "But we don't want to call any unnecessary attention to it, either. For one thing, our records show there's less fighting now between the hostile tribes than there has been for almost ten years. That's one thing we've been able to reduce."

"You take it as a good indication, then?" Ki asked.

"Not necessarily," the general replied. "Because some of the men analyzing the reports believe it means the Indians have put aside their tribal rivalries and are working together to mount a major campaign against the whites."

"I suppose you've had signs of that?" Jessie asked.

"We certainly have," Nesbitt nodded. "For one thing, the Indians now have a new, paganized kind of religion. One of their bucks—Wovoka's his name—has become something of a . . . well, I think the best short description of the man I can give you is to say he's a heathen evangelist."

"A preacher?" Jessie frowned.

"I'd call him that, yes," Nesbitt nodded. "Even though he's preaching from an unwritten gospel."

"What sort of message is he preaching?" Ki broke in to ask.

"From our standpoint I'm afraid it's not a good one," the general replied. "Wovoka claims that he's had visions, some sort of supernatural commands ordering the Indians to return to the old heathen ways. He's made up something he calls the Spirit Dance, and it's supposed to bring the ghosts of dead tribesmen back to life. Then the ghosts will guide the tribes back to the heathenish ways they had before the Indian Bureau was set up to civilize them."

"And the government doesn't want that to happen, I'm sure," Jessie said with a nod.

"Of course not!" the general replied quickly. "But as I said before, one thing we've noticed is that there's a lot less fighting between the different tribes than there was just a short while ago. And I've gathered an impression from the Indian Bureau reports I've read in the past several months that the Sioux Nation chiefs have met secretly two or three times."

"That doesn't necessarily mean they're planning to go to war, does it?" Jessie asked.

"Certainly not," he replied. "Although a number of us in the army have come to believe that this is just the beginning of some sort of arrangement between the tribes."

"An arrangement about what? Forgetting old tribal rivalries and joining together, uniting against new settlers?" Jessie asked.

"We've just about concluded that this Ghost Dance I mentioned is just one of the first steps they're taking toward forming some kind of an organization that will unite all the tribes on the western reservations."

"What kind of organization?" Ki asked, his usually expressionless face furrowed by an uncharacteristic frown.

"That's what our War Department experts on Indian fighting are trying to decide right now," Nesbitt replied. "Their idea at the moment is that at least a few of the young chiefs—those who've had some education in the Indian schools—are looking ahead to the time when they'll be leading their tribes."

"But you can't take that as a sign that they intend to start fighting," Jessie protested.

Nesbitt shook his head. "No. Not a certain sign, but it's far too early to tell much about anything such as that. But we must know about their plans. Our troops are spread very thin, Miss Starbuck, scattered at far too many western forts that should've been closed long ago."

"You're closing them now, I suppose?"

"As quickly as possible. We've taken the situation seriously enough to have the Signal Corps install a special system of buried telegraph lines between the remaining forts and the main Indian Bureau offices, so we can communicate with them in an emergency."

"Isn't that a bit extreme?" Jessie asked.

"Perhaps. But the line had been started, so we finished it as quickly as possible." The general shook his head and went on. "That's neither here nor there, Miss Starbuck. Now, I don't propose to give you orders, but old Fort Supply in the Indian Nation has been turned over to the Indian Bureau for a temporary headquarters. That seems to me to be the logical place for you to make your base."

"Do you think there'll be room for us, with the Indian Bureau using it?" Ki asked.

"That's a question I can't answer, Ki," Nesbitt answered. "Fort Supply's been built and partly razed and rebuilt several times, and I don't know how much it's changed since my last visit there, which was a number of years ago. There's talk of turning it over to the Indian Bureau as a permanent headquarters, but nothing's really been settled."

"We needn't worry about little details of that sort," Jessie said. "Let's get back to this job you want us to

48

do, General. In plain language, what you're asking us to do is look, watch, and listen. Am I correct?"

"Completely," the general nodded. "And to keep us informed in Washington about anything you consider significant."

"By the telegraph wire, I suppose?" Ki broke in to ask.

"Only if you encounter something important and urgent," Nesbitt answered. "We've kept our Signal Corps in charge of the telegraph wire, and I'll give you an order that will assure that you get clearance to use it if you need to."

"Being able to use the telegraph might turn out to be very handy," Jessie nodded. "But I won't use it unless it's for something really urgent."

"I'll also give you what we call a 'bearer' letter," the general went on. "It won't have your name on it, because I can foresee that there may be times when you'll need to assume a false identity."

"I've never heard of anything like that," Jessie said. "What's it used for?"

"Anything you choose," Nesbitt replied. "It simply requests all federal government officials and employees to give the bearer any assistance requested."

Jessie nodded her understanding as she said, "I'll be very careful about how I use it."

"I'm sure you will," Nesbitt said. "One thing more, now. I'd like to be kept informed by an occasional brief letter—even just a short note—giving your general impression of the Indian situation. Anything you learn about the new Ghost Dance, any hints as to the way the wind seems to be blowing."

"Do you need an answer right now, General?" Jessie asked. She was frowning thoughtfully as she spoke.

"I'm not under orders to act within any special length of time, or on any deadline. But I naturally want to complete my mission and report to the president that his instructions are being carried out."

"Of course," Jessie nodded.

She glanced at Ki. His expression had not changed. His features were totally bland and his nod responding to Jessie's unspoken query was almost imperceptible. She turned back to face General Nesbitt.

"I can't refuse your request, General," she said. "There are very few times when the president requests just an ordinary citizen to do something in service to our country."

"I wish more people felt that way," Nesbitt told her. "I'll notify the president just as soon as we get back to Fort Davis. Can I tell him that you'll be starting out soon?"

"It's more than likely that we'll be on our way before you get back to Fort Davis," Jessie told him. "It'll take us a day or so to get our travel gear ready because it's quite likely we'll be gone for several weeks. Also we'll have to stop over for a day in Fort Worth. I have some business to settle with my cattle broker."

"You'll be there a few days, I assume?" Nesbitt asked.

"Two or three, at least. Why do you ask?"

"I'll need to inform the general staff. They may want to send you some further instructions in care of the post there."

"But if they don't, we'll just follow the ones you're giving us?"

"As scanty as they are, yes," the general nodded.

"Then Ki and I will get some sort of outfit together and go on to the Indian Nation."

"You won't be leaving for a day or two, then?" Nesbitt asked.

"Probably the day after tomorrow," Jessie replied.

"I've caused you to go to a great deal of trouble, haven't I, Miss Starbuck?"

"Oh, I don't look at it that way, General," she replied. "One of the most valuable things my father taught me when I was growing up is that our country deserves to be served by everyone, even when it isn't easy."

"Your father was an unusual man," Nesbitt went on. "I had occasion to work with him a bit during the time when I was stationed at the Presidio in San Francisco."

"Then you'll know why I cherish his memory," Jessie said.

"Of course," the general nodded. "Your father was a very fine man. Now, if you'll excuse me, Miss Starbuck, I'll go back to my room and rest for a short while. I'm sure there must be some ranch business that you and Ki will want to discuss privately."

After Nesbitt had left the room, Jessie turned to Ki. She asked, "What's your opinion of the general's request, Ki?"

"I'm sure you were right in saying yes, Jessie," Ki replied. "You could hardly refuse to be of service to the president. But the job he wants us to do might turn into something more difficult than it appears to be when you're just talking about it."

"All I did was to think quickly what Alex would've done if he'd been sitting in my chair. The answer came automatically. And we've handled more difficult jobs, Ki. But I think that before we talk to the general again, you and I had better give a little thought to what we're

51

getting into, and get some sort of guidelines from him before we start out."

"That would be wise," Ki agreed. "Suppose you sit here and think of the things we'll need to know, while I take care of a few little chores. We'll put our heads together before we talk to General Nesbitt again."

Alone in the big room which Alex Starbuck had furnished with his usual impeccable taste, Jessie settled back into the soft leather seat of her favorite easy chair and closed her eyes as her head rested on its well-tanned back. Though several years had passed since her father's untimely death, a faint aroma of his pipe tobacco still clung to the glove-soft leather.

Alex had created the Circle Star as an isolated, peaceful haven where he could rest from the constant demands of his busy work life. Now, to Jessie, it offered the same refuge from her own busy life, for the extensive industrial and financial empire she'd inherited required from her the kind of continuous activity that had kept her father busy.

Alex's unaided efforts—unaided except for the jobs taken on by Ki—had made him one of America's richest men. His rise to wealth and power had not had an auspicious start. Alex's first venture after he'd decided that he was not cut out to be an Alaskan prospector had been a small curio store on San Francisco's waterfront. Thanks to his impeccable taste and an inborn sense of values, the store had prospered.

Needing a constant flow of fresh merchandise, Alex had started making regular trips to the Orient. There, at supper in a small restaurant where they had both dropped in for a meal, Alex had encountered Ki. At that time Ki was a freelance *karateka,* forced to make a marginal living by using the skills he'd learned in the *do*s of the masters of Oriental combat. Their meeting was fruitful for both men, since it led to Alex's discovery that Ki was the son of an officer in the United States Navy who had been one of Alex's closest friends.

Without the approval of his Japanese bride's noble family, Ki's father and mother had married, but both perished in a storm at sea when Ki was in his early youth. Disowned and cast out by his mother's family, Ki had drifted from one martial arts *do* to another. When Alex learned about the young man's history he'd offered Ki a job in his San Francisco curio shop. Ki accepted, and accompanied Alex on his return to the United States. During the years that followed, he became Alex's good right hand.

During the following years, Alex Starbuck's sure instinct and keen intelligence had kept him on a meteoric rise to great wealth. Small investments in stocks became richly rewarding ventures, real estate that he bought rose quickly in value, any investment he made seemed almost certain to prove successful.

Alex's first really large return, the purchase of a dilapidated shipyard near his small curio shop, had returned its purchase price a hundredfold. The money had provided Alex with the resources he'd needed to finance other ventures, and to exercise his Midas touch in other successful investments.

While still a relatively young man, Alex became one of America's richest men. His rise brought Alex invitations to join the finest clubs, and to participate in the most rewarding speculative ventures, such as stock-trading pools. It was a member of one such pool who tried to recruit Alex into a sinister underground cartel largely made up of European financiers. The cartel's secret objective was to capture the wealth of America and use its vast natural resources for the benefit of a lagging group of European nations.

Alex turned down the offer of this group of conspirators and began to combat the cartel. The few trusted associates he urged to join him refused, unable to believe that the secret, sinister group existed. Alex continued his battle alone—only Ki stayed at his side. During this period Alex married. To give his bride a safe haven he bought land in Southwest Texas and created the huge Circle Star Ranch.

Before the ranch could be completed, his beloved wife died giving birth to Jessie. Overcoming his grief, Alex completed the ranch and it was there where Jessie grew up. Alex entrusted her early upbringing to a wise old geisha whom Ki discovered in San Francisco's Oriental community.

Jessie was finishing her final term at an exclusive New England woman's academy when the cartel's hired killers finally succeeded in carrying out the cartel's aim to end Alex's efforts to destroy it. The murdering band staged a surprise raid on the Circle Star and brought Alex Starbuck down in a hail of bullets.

Ki had transferred to Jessie all the loyalty that he'd given Alex. He helped her to understand the intricacies of the vast holdings she'd inherited. When Jessie decided that she must carry on her father's fight to destroy the cartel, Ki joined her in fighting the vicious murdering group across most of Western America. When the cartel and its sinister masters were finally defeated, Jessie at last found peace and settled down at the Circle Star to oversee the industrial and financial empire that she'd inherited.

Now, leaning back in the chair which had been her father's favorite, Jessie thought of the task she'd been asked to do by the president. She knew the job would mean long periods of travel, hardship, and danger. She also knew that she could not have refused to serve her country. Closing her eyes, she began to think of the moves that she might need to make in order to carry out the job she'd accepted.

★

Chapter 5

"We've still got quite a way to travel, Ki," Jessie observed. "But time's not as important on this trip as it's been on so many that we've had to make."

"That's right," Ki agreed. "But when you have business with our cattle broker, it always takes longer than we've planned. Today's not likely to be any different."

"I'm counting on it being about the same," Jessie smiled. "And I'm sure I'll be tied up long enough to make it too late to start for the Indian Nation today, because we still have to buy the things on that list we made before we got off the train."

Jessie and Ki were sitting at breakfast in the dining room of the Stockman's Hotel in Fort Worth. Both of them had slept later than usual after getting off the train well after midnight following the long trip from the Circle Star, and a good part of the morning had already passed.

"Suppose I do some of our buying while you're at the cattle broker's office," Ki suggested. "I'm sure you'll want to choose the clothes you'll need to fit the part you plan to play."

"Certainly," Jessie agreed. "What I wear on the Circle Star wouldn't be suitable for the frumpy sort of woman I'm suppose to be, one who'd be traveling around the Indian Nation with—" she paused and smiled, "with an Oriental man as her companion."

"Of course not," Ki replied. "We've got to dress like the kind of people we're supposed to be. Of course, I don't need to worry about changing from what I always wear. There's a good side to look on, though."

"I can't think what it would be," Jessie frowned.

"Why, we know that we can count on finding everything we need here. If we finish our buying today we'll be able to start for the Indian Nation early tomorrow."

"I'm sure the time we spend shopping today will be well-spent," Jessie said. "General Nesbitt warned us that a lot of things are in short supply in the Nation, and this is the only town of any size left between us and the border."

Ki nodded, then went on thoughtfully, "We may have some trouble finding a horse and wagon that'll be sturdy but will look like they've both put a lot of miles behind them. And we'll need tools."

"Tools that'll show they've been used a lot," Jessie added. "I'll get some well-worn clothes from one of the hand-me-down stores."

"Why don't I take care of getting the tools while you're at the cattle broker's office?" Ki suggested. "And I'll buy some extra ammunition for your rifle and pistol."

"It'll certainly save time," Jessie agreed. As she stood up, she went on, "Suppose we meet here at the hotel at noon. That'll give us the rest of the day to finish our buying and arrange to rent a horse and wagon. If we can't find them for rent, we'll just buy the kind we need."

Ki nodded as he said, "We can get everything we need before the day's out. Then we'll make an early start tomorrow and be about halfway to the Indian Nation by the time we have to stop for the night."

From their regular trips to cattle sales at the big Fort Worth stockyards, both Jessie and Ki were familiar with the streets of the fast-growing town. Jessie headed for the newly developed commercial area, Ki for the older decaying section which was now being taken over by secondhand stores, saloons, and rooming houses.

There was no reason for Ki to hurry, and he took his time. After he reached the slowly decaying older section of the town he strolled along the street at a leisurely pace. He paused at each of the secondhand stores that occupied one of the dilapidated buildings, peering through their grime-crusted windows, inspecting their stock.

Although he went into a few which had windows so dirty that the contents could not be seen clearly, Ki wasted no time after his quick glances around the interiors. Almost all the merchandise displayed seemed to consist of chipped china, marginally usable farm tools, and tattered well-worn secondhand clothing. He made mental notes of the most promising stores.

Ki reached a shop sandwiched between two vacant buildings, and when he saw that the windows had recently been washed he stopped to peer inside. Through the shining glass he could see that the store's racks of used clothing had been neatly sorted. Stacks of chinaware rose from the tops of two tables near the center of the room, and the tools that lined one wall appeared to be in better condition than most of those which he'd inspected.

A woman was standing behind a counter that spanned the rear wall of the shop, talking to a man who faced her on the opposite side. Deciding he'd at last found a place that gave promise of yielding something that he might be seeking he stepped through the shop's door.

As usual, Ki had on the supple soft-soled slippers that he favored. They made only a whisper of noise as he entered. He was halfway to the counter when the man standing in front of it turned. Only then did Ki realize that he'd interrupted a robbery in progress, for as the man swiveled around he flourished the nickle-plated revolver which he'd been aiming at the young woman behind the counter.

"Git your damn hands up!" the holdup man snarled. "And keep 'em high, if you know what's good for you! There ain't no Chink alive that can keep me from finishing a job I start!"

Ki started to raise his arms, but as he brought them up he was measuring with expert eyes the distance between him and the holdup man. He knew that the bandit's attention would be distracted momentarily by following the movements of his arms. That split second was all Ki needed.

As the holdup man's eyes flicked upward, Ki swiveled on the heel of one foot and arched his torso backward. While his foot was rising he gauged the sweep that would be needed for his upraised foot to land on the outlaw's head at the end of the *kakato-geri* attack.

In the fraction of a second that elapsed between the time the bandit turned and Ki launched his surprise attack, the holdup man did not have time to trigger off a shot. Ki's heel landed on the man's head. The impact sent the bandit staggering sidewise in a reeling fall. His trigger finger closed in a reflexive reaction to the blow he'd taken. Belatedly, the pistol barked, but the robber's gun hand was already sagging, dragged down by the weight of his weapon. The slug from the drooping revolver plowed a short crease in the wooden floor and whistled through the door.

During the brief moment while the pistol shot still echoed in the store, the bandit was slumping to the floor. His eyes were glazed and rolling from Ki's *kakato-geri* kick. The revolver dropped from his hand and thunked on the floor as his knees bent. Then he lurched and fell in a heap, huddled in a motionless daze. Before the outlaw could recover, Ki pounced on his recumbent form. Grabbing the collar of the man's shirt, Ki pulled it downward in back until the folds of the shirt were clustered at the outlaw's elbows. The fabric bound his arms as effectively as though they'd been tied with a rope.

"Just stay right still where you're at!" a man's voice sounded from the doorway. "I got you covered, and I got a nervous trigger finger!"

Glancing up, Ki saw a uniformed policeman standing in the doorway. The officer was holding his revolver in a steady hand, swiveling it slowly to cover both Ki and the woman while he flicked his eyes around the store's interior. Then the woman behind the counter spoke for the first time.

"Leave the Chinaman alone!" she called to the policeman. "He's the one that saved me from being robbed and maybe shot by that outlaw laying there!"

"I'd just come through the door when I saw what was happening," Ki volunteered. "That fellow on the floor fired a shot at me and missed, and I protected myself."

"I heard that shot and come a-running," the officer said. "But it looks like you done a pretty good job. And if that's the way it was, I better take care of this crook before he comes around."

As he spoke the policeman was pulling handcuffs from his belt. He bent over the still-dazed holdup man and snapped the shackles around the recumbent man's wrists. The outlaw was coming out of his daze now. He tried to use his hands to lever himself up from the floor. When he fell back and realized belatedly what had happened, he started swearing.

"Shut your damn mouth!" the policeman ordered. He turned back to Ki and the woman, and went on, "You two wait here. I better get this yahoo down to the call box at the corner and signal for the paddy wagon. I'll have to wait till the wagon gets there, but I'll be back after I take him to the station and book him into jail."

"That's going to take quite a bit of time," Ki said. "And I have business to take care of. You know you can find this lady here whenever she's needed for a statement or to sign papers filing a charge against that fellow."

"How about you?" the officer asked. "I'll want a statement from you too."

"I will be glad to stop at the station later to give you one," Ki suggested. "My name is Ki, and I am stopping at the Stockman's Hotel."

"I guess that'll be all right," the officer agreed. He bent to grasp the frustrated holdup man's arm and lift him to his feet. "I'll get him started for the lockup, then."

As the policeman hustled the bandit from the store, the young woman behind the counter turned to Ki and breathed a sigh. She said, "I'm glad that's over with. I heard you tell the policeman your name. Mine's Clarisse."

"I'm glad to know you, Clarisse," Ki told her as he made one of his half-bows. "And I am also glad that I was here to help you."

"This is the most excitement I've had for a long time," Clarisse said. "I need a swallow of coffee to settle down my nerves, Ki. I keep a pot warm in the back room, if you'd like to have some too."

Although Ki would have preferred tea, he smiled as he replied, "That would be very pleasant."

Clarisse gestured for him to come with her and turned toward a door behind the counter. Ki moved around the counter and followed her into a room almost as large as the store. A rumpled bed showing signs that it had been spread hurriedly took up one corner of the room, a stove with a coffeepot on its surface filled another corner. A table stood close to the stove, chinaware on a wall shelf above it. Along the opposite wall clothing hung on a rack. Two chairs and a small dressing table completed the room's furnishings.

"I haven't had a chance to redd up," Clarisse apologized as she reached to the shelf for cups and saucers. "I've been trying to get things decent back here and fix up the store at the same time. I haven't really been here long enough to settle in."

"Then you've just bought the store?" Ki asked.

"Not bought," she replied. "My uncle left it to me in his will. He died about a month or so ago."

While she talked, Clarisse was taking cups and saucers from the shelf and placing them on the table. She stepped to the stove and picked up the coffeepot, filled the cups, and gestured for Ki to sit down.

After she'd settled at the table Clarisse went on, "You know, Ki, I sure owe you for stopping that stickup man. I need what little money I've got on hand a lot worse than he did."

"You owe me nothing," Ki assured her. "I'm very glad that I happened to stop at your store in time to help."

"Whatever you're looking for is likely in the barn out in back. There's all sorts of truck in it, tools and rope and tents and things like that."

"It sounds like you might have some things I've been looking for along the street here," Ki told her. "It was just luck that I got here when I did."

"You couldn't've picked a better time," Clarisse smiled. "And I noticed you're not toting anything, so I guess you're still looking for whatever you're after. You're likely to find most anything out in the barn. It's just a step or two from the back door, there. If you want to look, I can close the front door and go out and maybe help you."

"Suppose you show me the way and I'll look around while our coffee's cooling," Ki suggested. "You should be in here in case another customer comes in. If I find something I want, I can bring it in here for you to set a price."

"That's right thoughtful, Ki," she smiled. "But business isn't all that good. I'll go with you, and if you find anything you can use, I'll make you a real good price on it."

When Clarisse unlocked the padlock and Ki helped her open the wide double doors of the barn he saw such an assortment of articles that for a moment he stood blinking in astonishment. The heaps of goods inside were covered by a heavy film of dust, but as his eyes became accustomed to the gloomy interior he began to distinguish details.

In the barely visible array there were axes, rakes, hoes, shovels, harness, saddles, cooking utensils, chairs, tables, bed frames, crutches, canes. There were single worn boots as well as pairs, stacks of china and glassware, bottles, jugs, buckets, and a number of unidentifiable shapeless heaps in the dim rear interior of the building. Some were so thickly covered with dust that Ki could only guess what was hidden by the grime.

"It's a real mess, isn't it?" Clarisse asked.

"I suppose that's the best way to describe it," he agreed.

Clarisse went on, "Uncle Nate bought just about everything folks brought in to sell. I've just started to sort it all out so that when somebody comes looking for something I can find it."

"I'd say you've got a long job ahead," Ki told her.

"Oh, I know that," she nodded. "But it's better than being a saloon girl. Now, our coffee's getting cold, we'd better drink it before you start looking."

"Even after such a short look, I'm sure you've got just about everything I'm looking for except a wagon."

"There's a two-horse wagon buried under that pile of pots and pans over there," Clarisse said, pointing. She smiled and went on, "I don't have the horses to pull it, but I've got the harness."

"It'll take me a bit of time to look around," Ki said. "Let's drink our coffee. Then I'll come back and start picking out what I'll need."

Seated again at the kitchen table, freshly poured coffee in their cups, Clarisse looked at Ki and a puzzled frown formed on her face as she said, "Can I ask you a question, Ki?"

"Of course."

"Why do you want all these things you're looking for?"

"I work for a lady who owns a ranch down in Southwest Texas. We're going to the Indian Nation."

"Now I understand why you want all the things you're looking for," she said. "Are you going to stay there?"

"Just for a short while." Ki stood up as he spoke.

Clarisse extended her hand as though asking him to help her to her feet. Ki grasped her hand. As she stood up she made a half-turn to wrap his arm around her in an embrace. Clarisse was facing him now, pressing her body against him. She turned her face up, offering her lips.

Ki leaned toward her, accepting her invitation. A moment after their lips met and pressed he felt the tip of her questing tongue and met it with his own. Then her hand began exploring his crotch, and after his long spell of abstinence on the Circle Star, Ki did not try to suppress the erection that soon followed her finger-play.

He responded to her invitation by caressing her full breasts softly, fingering them and feeling their tips grow firm in response to his gentle touches. Clarisse's body began to quiver, soft ripples that he could feel through their clothing.

Twisting her head to break their kiss, Clarisse said, "The bed's waiting for us, Ki. Let's don't waste any more time."

Ki was ready enough by now. He edged out of Clarisse's arms and began to push the wide neckline of her dress down her shoulders. She shrugged to help him, and only seconds passed before the dress rippled to the floor. Clarisse wore nothing under the dress. She threw her shoulders back, and Ki bent to press his lips on the soft, pink rosettes of her generous breasts and to caress them with the tip of his tongue.

Clarisse began to sigh, a gentle throaty murmur of pleasure, as Ki's head moved back and forth between the soft smooth mounds and his tongue explored their pink, pebbled, protruding tips. Her busy hands had crept past the waistband of Ki's loose trousers now and were fumbling at the overlapping folds of his *cache-sex*. She found the tucked-under end of the long linen strip and tugged it away. Then her fingers closed on Ki's firm erect flesh as she began to fondle and squeeze him.

After a moment had passed Clarisse shrugged her shoulders and Ki raised his head. She nodded toward the bed. Ki wrapped his arms around her and lifted his feet from the floor long enough to kick his trousers away. He lifted her feet from the floor and carried her to the bed.

"Wait!" Clarisse whispered.

Ki stopped at the bedside. She brought up her legs and in the moment before locking them behind Ki's back Clarisse slid her hand between their bodies to place him.

"Now!" Clarisse urged.

Ki bent to let Clarisse fall backward, falling with her to retain their fleshly connection. A wordless gasp burst from her throat as Ki completed his penetration. The gasp became a small, happy cry as he lunged in his first lusty lunge, then Clarisse locked her feet above his back and brought her hips up to meet him. Bubbling sighs of pleasure began bursting from her throat when Ki started thrusting slowly and deliberately.

After Ki had maintained his steady, measured driving for several moments, Clarisse caught his rhythm. She began bringing her hips up, twisting them from one side to the other. Ki did not hurry. Now and then he held himself deeply buried for a few moments until Clarisse silently suggested by twisting her hips that she wanted him to resume his thrusts. Suddenly she began to tremble, and Ki speeded his lunges to a faster pace.

As the tremors of his body shook her at shorter and shorter intervals he stopped now and then, buried deeply, until her quivers subsided. When Clarisse's undulating shivers shook her at shorter and shorter intervals he began once more to increase the tempo of his thrusting.

As the moments passed, Clarisse began to quiver almost constantly. Ki thrust with slowly mounting speed until he felt her soft body suddenly grow tense and the tempo of her shudders give way to sudden lusty gyrations. Ki read her signs and began to drive. He no longer thrust gently, but increased his tempo to trip-hammer speed.

Clarisse cried out, a long half-stifled moan, and the pace of her response to Ki's thrusts grew raggedly spastic. Then she screamed softly as her hips began to gyrate wildly. Now Ki began pounding, driving fiercely, until she cried out in smothered gasps of pleasure attained. He went in deeply and held himself to her until Clarisse suddenly went limp and lay shuddering for a moment, her voice rasping now with dying sighs.

Ki stopped thrusting and held himself buried in her warmly pulsing depths.

"I hope you feel as good as I do," Clarisse whispered.

"Yes, very good indeed," he answered. "And ready to start again whenever you are."

"Again?" she gasped. "So soon?"

"Suit your pleasure," he told her. "I can wait."

"Oh, I won't make you wait," she replied. "Start any time. I'd like nothing better than to stay here the rest of the day."

"We'll make the most of the time we have," Ki said. "And even if it's all too short we'll both have this pleasure to remember."

★

Chapter 6

"We'd better let the team rest here for a few minutes," Ki told Jessie. "There wasn't much current, but they're tired from pulling their hooves out of that mud on the bottom."

He was tugging the reins to bring the panting horses to a halt. Behind them on the greenish surface of the stream the bubbled muddy froth remaining on the surface after their crossing was slowly stringing out on the sluggish current and vanishing. Droplets of muddy water were still running off the haunches and legs of both horses as well as off the wagon wheels.

"Yes, the horses certainly do need it after the struggle they had with that soft bottom the river has along here," Jessie agreed. "There were a couple of times when I thought we were going to bog down."

Ki nodded. "The Canadian's not very much of a river this far upstream, but that deep mud really puts a strain on a team pulling a loaded wagon across it."

"It hasn't been as bad a trip as I'd thought it would, though," Jessie remarked, watching Ki as he wrapped the leathers around the whipsocket beside the wagon's dashboard.

"We've been lucky," Ki reminded her. "I really didn't have much hope for this wagon when I first looked at it, but the old wheelwright in Fort Worth put it into really good shape."

"And it's certainly gotten us over some rough road," Jessie said. She began scanning the almost straight line of the horizon. "We can't be too far from Fort Supply now, but I suppose that this kind of country's close kin to the Circle Star range: everything you look at seems to be a lot closer than it really is."

Swiveling on the wagon seat, Jessie stepped up on it to look at the terrain ahead. As far as she could see, the prairie was barren. Beyond the twin strips of greenery that bordered each bank of the winding river they'd just crossed, waist-high swathes of grass stretched to the horizon.

"I don't think we'll have any more trouble," Ki told her as he stepped up on the seat to join her. "All of that stretch ahead looks pretty level, and we don't have much further to go. We should get to Fort Supply by tomorrow afternoon."

Jessie and Ki were looking at an almost treeless country. Here and there a small straggling stand of low-growing trees, the largest only a little higher than saplings, rose to break the skyline. In some spots of the generally featureless prairie the yellowing grass was belly-high to a horse, but these were the exception to the generally barren nature of the land. Except for the green growth bordering the river, the grass was sparse and short, yellowed, and drying everywhere else on the seemingly endless stretch of prairie that surrounded them.

"I feel better now that we're across the Canadian," Jessie said. "It's the last big river we'll have to cross before we get to Fort Supply. And judging by what we can see from here, all there is ahead of us is the same kind of country we've been traveling over from—"

Jessie broke off as a distant shot broke the silence of the windless air. She started swiveling her head to follow the horizon line, and far to the west of their position she pointed to four black moving shapes outlined against the sky.

"They can't be shooting at us," she said as Ki turned his head to look in the direction she'd indicated. "We're out of range, and as far as I know there's nobody here in the Indian Nation who has any grudges against us, even if they could recognize us this far away from them."

Jessie had barely finished speaking when another spate of scattered shooting sounded. The four riders veered as the shots filled the air with their distant reports. Now they were heading directly toward Jessie and Ki. Then the horizon beyond the approaching horsemen was broken by another string of mounted men. A puff of gun smoke rose above the heads of the second band, and the report of the shot echoed faintly.

"We know what we're watching now," Ki said. "Or we can make a pretty good guess."

"A posse chasing outlaws, I'd say," Jessie told him.

"That's all it could be," Ki nodded. "And unless those men in front decide to scatter and break away from that straight line, they seem to be following toward us. There's not much we can do to keep clear of the trouble that's sure to be coming."

73

"It's not our fight, Ki," Jessie pointed out. "Let's be smart and not get mixed up in it."

Ki slapped the reins on the back of the team, and as the animals started ahead he tightened one of the leathers to turn the wagon on a course paralleling the riverbed. They'd covered only a short distance before a fresh rattle of shots broke the air and one of the four riders between the wagon and the pursuing horsemen suddenly reared back in his saddle and dropped to the ground.

More shots from the second group followed. The front-riders were close to the river now. Suddenly one of them reined in, and as his horse reared to a stop the man raised his hands above his head. Within the next few moments his companions followed suit. The horsemen in pursuit soon reached their quarry, and for a few minutes the two bands merged as they dismounted. Jessie and Ki could see little now except the mixture of men and horses.

"We might as well get back on the trail again," Jessie suggested. "Now that the fighting's stopped, we can just keep going in the direction we should be following."

"It looks like the shooting's over," said Jessie as she and Ki settled back on the wagon seat and watched the two groups of riders in front of them merging and mingling. "Even if we're pretty sure our guesses about those two bunches are right, we're going to have a visit from one of them," said Ki.

Jessie turned to look at the merged group of horsemen. One of them had detached himself from the others and was riding toward them. She and Ki watched silently while the man approached. He wore a fore-and-aft-creased Stetson and was in his shirtsleeves. As he drew near they could see that he sported an oversize moustache, a mixture of dark hair and grey. He was cradling his left forearm against his chest. When he got even closer they saw that the shirtsleeve of the arm he favored was stained with blood. There was also a bloodstain on the front of his white shirt.

"Nothing to get all spooked up about, folks," he called as soon as he was within easy speaking distance. He reined up when he reached the wagon and doffed his Stetson when he saw Jessie. He went on, "My name's Heck Thomas, I'm a deputy sheriff from Lawton, that's a little ways over to the west of here. Me and them other fellows have been chasing that outlaw bunch since right after daybreak. I hope all the shooting us and them was doing didn't stir you up too bad."

"It didn't," Jessie replied quickly. "We've both heard shooting before, we aren't tenderfeet. I'm Jessica Starbuck and this is Ki. I have a ranch down in Southwest Texas where we have a little trouble now and then, so we've learned to keep clear of other people's fights."

"Oh, the fighting's all finished now," Thomas said. "I reckon you seen them other outlaws give up. While my posse's loading that dead outlaw on a horse and tying up the others, I rode over here to find out if you folks might have some kinda clean rags I could put on for a bandage."

"Of course we have," Jessie replied quickly. "And some antiseptic as well. That looks like a bad wound you've got."

"Well, I been hurt worse," Thomas told her. "But I got to admit I rode over here because I figured you folks might have something better than a wad of chewing tobacco in a bandanna to sorta fix me up with."

Ki was already on his feet and stepping over the back of the seat to the wagon bed. He volunteered, "I'll get what we need to bandage Mr. Thomas's arm, Jessie."

Jessie nodded, then turned back to Thomas to ask, "I suppose that outlaw you shot was a really bad one?"

"He was that, ma'am. Aaron Purdy's his name. Him and his bunch robbed a train at the Snake Creek crossing and killed two of the railroaders. He was slick enough to get away and pull his bunch of no-goods together, but they left a trail a one-eyed jackass wouldn't've had no trouble following, so we finally caught up with 'em."

Ki returned with some strips of cloth and a bottle of colorless liquid. As he moistened the cloth he said, "This is the best thing we've found to use, Mr. Thomas, a clean cloth bandage soaked in pure alcohol."

"We'll have you bandaged very quickly," Jessie told him. "On the ranch Ki and I have to fix up wounds every now and then." She went on, "Now, I'll sit down and let Ki bandage you. He's far better than I am at such things."

Except for an occasional involuntary grunt of pain, the wounded lawman did not move or complain while Ki did the bandaging quickly and silently. Jessie neither moved nor looked back until she heard him say, "This is about all I can do for you out here on the prairie, Marshal Thomas. But I'm sure that when you get to the nearest town, or perhaps the first army fort you come to, you'll want to go to a doctor and have him look at that chest wound."

"Oh, I'll be all right," Thomas replied. "But if it festers or I get sore later on, I'll find me a sawbones."

"I hope you don't have far to ride," Jessie said. She looked at the horsemen who were waiting for Thomas. They'd put the dead outlaw's body across his horse and were sitting in their saddles gazing toward the wagon.

"It ain't all that far, ma'am. I'm still a little bit sore, but I'll be all right. Thank you kindly for your help. Maybe I can give you a hand sometimes."

Mounting his horse, Thomas touched his hat and rode off to join his companions. Jessie turned to Ki and shook her head.

"I wish there were a lot more like him left," she said. "Alex used to say that the old-time cowboy breed was thinning out, and we're seeing the truth of that right now."

"Your father was right about almost everything," Ki nodded. "But we'd better start moving again, Jessie. It's still a good two-day trip from here to Fort Supply."

"Just looking at this place, you'd think the Indians were the winners in all the fighting that was done to open the West to settlers, Ki," Jessie remarked.

"All you have to do is look at the teepees along the riverbank down there to see that," Ki replied.

"Let's just sit here for a minute or two and get some idea of how the land lays," Jessie suggested. "The horses need to rest a few minutes after that long uphill haul, and we'd better have some idea of what the land's like around the fort."

Ki pulled up the team and they settled back in the wagon seat, surveying the almost circular valley that fell away from the crest they'd reached. After his first sweeping glance, he turned to Jessie.

"This is as good a spot as any," Ki said. "But in spite of the river going right by it, I don't think much of it as a location for a fort. And the Indians seem to've taken over every inch of land on both sides of the stream. General Nesbitt couldn't've seen this place lately or he wouldn't've suggested that we use it as our headquarters."

"There's not much of the original fort left," Jessie went on. "I remember seeing some pictures of it in Frank Leslie's weekly magazine when I was just a little girl, or I might not have recognized it."

She was still studying the valley, gazing at the cone-shaped tepees that in all directions engulfed and surrounded the remains of what in the fort's earlier days had been its stockade. Although more than half of its walls were in ruins now, Jessie could see that in its original form the fort had been enclosed in a high barricade, a square formed by setting logs upright into the ground. Now there were wide gaps in the once-sturdy enclosure. Only the high, square lookout stations that rose above the outer wall at each corner remained reasonably intact.

Inside the area defined by the lookout stations there was a huddle of six sheds and five large buildings, which Jessie took to be barracks. The largest one seemed to be a mess hall. All the buildings were still intact, and they dwarfed the ramshackle sheds that were dotted around them and the scores of conical tepees that stretched away from the old fort's buildings and filled almost every inch of ground in the remaining area of the saucerlike depression.

There were so many that Jessie did not even try to count them. They were crowded very closely against one another. The tepees did not stop at what remained of the old walls of the fort. They extended almost to the rim of the upsloping volcanic crater. At the point where

Jessie and Ki had stopped, the nearest tepees were less than a hundred yards distant.

"I don't think I've ever seen so many tepees in one place before, Ki," Jessie remarked without taking her eyes off the depression. "There must be several hundred of them here."

"I haven't even tried to count them," Ki told her. "But your guess is certainly a close one."

"Do you think they'll let us pitch our tent down there?"

"It's hard to say," he replied. "All we can do is try to find some space that isn't claimed by one of the Indians."

"We need to be close to them, of course," Jessie went on, her voice thoughtful. "And from what General Nesbitt told us, the Indians aren't exactly friendly right at this moment."

"What we'd better do first is find out who's in charge of things here," Ki suggested.

"From the way things look, the Indians are in charge," Jessie smiled. "But surely there'll be some Indian Bureau official who's responsible for the government people." She gestured toward the largest of the adobe buildings. "Just at a guess—that must be the headquarters."

"It looks like it might be," Ki agreed. "Most government bureaucrats like to impress the public by having their offices in the biggest buildings."

"So I've noticed," Jessie smiled. "Let's go see if our guess is right."

Ki slapped the reins over the team's backs and the horses began plodding ahead. He let them pick their own path most of the time, touching the reins only when it became necessary to keep them on a fairly straight course. They passed through the scattered tepees on the fringes of the encampment, the few Indians around paying them little attention except for an occasional searching stare.

"We're not going to be able to get the wagon through that maze of tepees up ahead," Ki said after they'd covered half the distance to the fort's buildings. He gestured toward the tepees in front of them, which stood cheek by jowl with little room and no visible paths between them. "I certainly wouldn't want to leave it unguarded, even if we were just outside the headquarters."

"You're right about that," Jessie agreed. She gestured toward a small unoccupied spot just ahead as she went on, "That's as good a place as any to stop, I suppose. Why don't you stay with the wagon while I walk the rest of the way by myself. I'll admit I'm curious to find out how we'll be greeted and treated in our new identities."

"And I've got to remember that you're now Jessie Star," Ki smiled. "And while we're talking about your new name, one of the things we've mentioned but never have talked out is what we'll do if we run into somebody who recognizes you and gives your real name away."

"I think the only thing we can do is bluff." Jessie frowned as Ki reined the wagon to a halt. "It's certainly something that we can't control or foresee. And I'm sure we'll be able to handle a situation like that. We've faced much worse."

Jessie was getting out of the wagon as she spoke. She stood beside it for a moment to orient herself, then started toward the big building, still a sizable distance away.

As she wove in and out between the tepees, the Indians scattered around them paid little or no attention to her, acting as though strangers were no novelty. Most of them were engrossed in business of their own—the women cooking or mending clothing, the men in low-voiced conversations with one another.

In front of several of the tepees small groups of men were hunkered down around outspread blankets or tanned animal skins, gambling. Jessie was familiar with the most common of the games, the stick game. It was played in much the same fashion as throwing dice, the players using small rectangles of polished wood marked with dots on each side.

She saw very little money exchanging hands. Trade script, rifle bullets, and knives were the common currency; tanned pelts from coyotes and occasionally a wolf skin also appeared now and then. In one of the games, an old, crease-skinned Indian used an elaborate feathered war bonnet for currency. It lay on the gaming skin, and he kept one hand on it while he threw the marker-sticks.

Though her walk did not cover a great distance, the zigzags and detours that she was forced to make around the tepees, and the need to skirt—and on more than one occasion to push her way—through an occasional large group of Indians made Jessie's walk seem almost endless. Threading a zigzag course among the Indians who were lounging in front of the building, Jessie started pushing and dodging until she reached the door.

Inside the building the chaos was compounded. As Jessie looked around she could see the loose ends of boards and wall studs that showed how the big structure had at one time been divided into a number of rooms. Most of the partitioning walls had been

81

removed, leaving only a few small rooms at one end. A long counter stretched across the big room. A line of Indians extending almost to the outer wall stood in front of the counter, behind which some clerks were busy with tablets and stacks of papers.

Other Indians were clustered along the walls and in small groups scattered around the floor. Between their talking and the talking coming from the lines around the counter, the noise in the cavernous interior was almost deafening. It was a confused gaggle of sound that echoed from the ceiling and bare walls and seemed to find its focal center just past the doorway. Whether they were entering or leaving, the Indians she encountered paid little attention to her, acting as though strangers were no novelty and merited no notice.

At last Jessie reached the long counter that spanned the big, echoing room. By this time she'd become accustomed to pushing her way ahead. A middle-aged man who was working at the end of the counter had no line waiting in front of him. He was bending over the counter thumbing through a sheaf papers. She edged her way along it and stopped in front of him.

"Pardon me," she said when he did not look up. "I'd like to get some information."

"If it's a grub-ration you're after, you got to get in line," he replied without interrupting his search through the papers in front of him. "Somebody'll tell you what tribe goes where in the ration lines."

"I'm not looking for food," she explained. "I want to know where I can pitch a tent."

"Find out where your tribe is and pick out any place big enough," the clerk said. He still did not raise his head.

"I don't belong to any tribe," Jessie replied, putting a rein on her growing irritation. "I want to—"

"Holy Samantha!" the man broke in as he looked up for the first time. "Why, you're a white woman!"

"I'm not quite sure who or what you were expecting to see," Jessie told him. "But I want to talk for a moment with someone who can answer a few questions."

"What kind of questions?" the clerk asked.

"Questions about Indians, of course," Jessie replied. She fell back on the scheme that she and Ki had devised to cover their activities while in the Indian Nation so that they could move freely without arousing too much curiosity. "I've come here to study them and talk to them to get the information I need to write a book about them."

"A book about the redskins?" the clerk gasped as he stared at her with his mouth opened in surprise. "Who'd want to do a thing like that?"

"I would, for one," she said. Her voice was a bit tart. "Now will you please tell me the proper person to give me the information I'm after?"

"Well, I reckon the man you better see is Rafe Corbett. He's in charge of this agency, and I guess he knows about as much as anybody about what you're looking for. But I'll tell you this without you asking. He sure ain't going to like it."

★

Chapter 7

For a moment Jessie stared at the man behind the counter. Then she asked, "Why do you say that?"

"Because—" the clerk stopped short. He peered around the room, then leaned toward her and dropped his voice as he replied, "Because Rafe's got a temper that's hotter than a fire in a blast furnace and he don't like people bothering him while he's busy."

"How do you know he's busy? Can you see his office from here?"

Jessie was scanning the big room as she spoke. Extending from the two end walls of the big building were short rows of closed doors, but if there were names on any of them the distance was too great for her to read the lettering.

"Rafe's always busy, or he sure acts like he is," the man behind the counter told her. He nodded in the direction of the nearest side wall. "But since you asked, that's his office over yonder."

"Does he have an office behind each door?" she asked.

"No, but he'd sure like to have. Rafe ain't the kinda man that shorts himself. You'll find him in the one at the far end there. But—" the man suddenly stopped.

Jessie waited for him to continue and when he remained silent she asked, "But what?"

"Never mind, ma'am. What I was about to say don't matter. I ain't even supposed to be talking to nobody but the Indians. Rafe don't like for us to go palavering with strangers. I hope you won't tell him I said that, though."

"I won't," Jessie said. "But I'm curious to know why you asked me not to."

"You ain't going to find him the easiest man in the world to get along with. He really don't take kindly to much of anything, but you'll be doing me a favor if you don't let him know it was me that showed you where to find him."

"I'll be careful not to mention it," Jessie promised. "And I appreciate the help you've given me."

"It's a pleasure, ma'am," the clerk nodded. "Just talking to somebody besides a redskin. And I'll be looking out for that book you're going to write."

Jessie wasted no time. She turned away from the counter, stepping fast to get clear of the Indians who'd queued up to form a line behind her and were pushing against her. Then she began picking her way through the crowd of Indians, trying vainly to follow a straight path to the door of the superintendent's office.

When Jessie's first tapping on the door brought no response, she knocked again. This time a man's gruff voice replied, "Door's not locked. Come on in."

Jessie's first glance at the Indian Bureau superintendent confirmed the impression that his voice had created when he replied to her knock. Corbett was sitting in a swivel chair, tilted back with his booted feet on a desk; they were almost buried by the piles of papers scattered on its surface. He was a bulky man, broad in the shoulders and bulging at the waist.

The hands he clasped over his belly-hump were like small, red hams; his cheeks were high and chubby beneath thick, bristling red eyebrows that duplicated the sandy hue of his short-cropped hair. His cold blue eyes seemed small in the flesh that bulked up from the mounds of his cheeks. His chin was buried in two rolls of fat on his jowls.

"Well?" he asked. His coarse, grating voice seemed to come from his throat as he went on. "Who are you and what do you want?"

"My name is Jessie Star, Mr. Corbett," she replied, using for the first time the name she'd assumed for her role during the investigation. "I'm thinking of writing a book about Indians, and I've come here looking for material."

"You're sure you don't work for one of them damn lying newspapers and you're here trying to dig up some scandal?" he asked. His voice was hoarse and grating.

"Scandal is not my field," Jessie replied. "Now, I've been told that you're in charge of everything here in the Indian Nation—I'm hoping you'll give me some advice from time to time. I've already learned that I'll need to find out a lot of details about Indians before I begin writing anything."

Corbett did not reply for a long moment, then he leaned to one side and spat a wad of tobacco and a generous dowsing of brown spittle into a cuspidor that stood on the floor a short distance from the end of his desk.

"I'll give you the best advice you're likely to get," he told Jessie, "before you start plaguing my Indians and getting 'em all stirred up."

"I certainly don't intend to stir up any trouble with the Indians, and I'll be be glad to get your advice," she replied.

"Turn around and go back to wherever it is you come from," Corbett said. "I got enough to worry about with four thousand redskins spread out from here to hell and gone. I don't have time to waste wet-nursing a time-waster, whether it's you or somebody else with some harebrained scheme."

Although Jessie had not expected to be greeted with any show of enthusiasm, Corbett's hostile bluntness came as a surprise. She kept her face expressionless and her voice neutral as she answered, "I'm sorry to hear you say that, Mr. Corbett. I hadn't expected any sort of warm welcome, either from you or the Indians, but neither had I looked to be—well, told quite so bluntly that I'm not a welcome visitor."

"Now that you've found out, what're you going to do?"

"I'm afraid I don't understand what you're asking," she said.

His voice carrying an unspoken challenge, Corbett said, "I'm not asking, Miss Star. I'm telling. I've got no time to waste on whatever new trouble that you'd likely start if you go snooping around bothering my Indians. It's enough of a job to keep 'em quieted down and peaceful as it is, and you better take my word on that."

"I can't see how anything I might do or say would cause you any trouble," Jessie frowned.

"You don't know as much about these redskins as I do. They've got all sorts of secret things they set store by, things that go way back. They don't take kindly to strangers—white strangers especially—who go poking at them with a bunch of damn fool questions."

"I'd certainly be careful about the questions I'll need to ask," Jessie assured him.

"Careful won't cut bacon," Corbett snapped. His voice took on a note of challenge as he went on, "What you better do is just turn right around and go back to wherever it is you've come from before I have you sent back."

Jessie took her time replying. She waited until Corbett started tapping his fingertips on the desk top before she said, "I'll go ahead with my plans, of course. I don't believe that in spite of your position you have more power than the governor of any other state or territory. The United States is a free country, and not even the president has a right to banish a citizen from any part of it. Neither do you."

"Now, you listen here," Corbett commanded. His face was now a shade or two redder than it had been, and his bushy eyebrows were pulled together in a scowl. "I'm the boss in this place. When I say diddley, folks squat. I don't guess I can stop you from noseying around, but if you get the redskins riled up, bothering 'em, you'll be sorry."

Jessie did not wish to exasperate the Indian agent any further. She said, "This conversation is getting us nowhere, Mr. Corbett. I don't wish to anger you, but as I told you a moment ago, I intend to stay here long enough to ask the questions I must have answered. I have no intention of interfering with you or your clerks, if that's what you call them. I don't intend to cause you any trouble, but—"

She stopped short as Corbett broke in to say, "Lady, I've got troubles you don't know anything about, and you don't know what trouble is till you get crossways of me."

He paused, his eyes locked with Jessie's, trying to stare her down, but she met his gaze without changing her expression. It was Corbett who dropped his eyes first.

"I'll go this far," he said. "As long as you stay out from underfoot and don't get the redskins roiled up, I won't stand in your way. But I can promise you one thing. If you make any sort of trouble for me, you'll be awful sorry."

Jessie did not respond to the Indian agent's threat for a moment while she phrased her reply. Then she said calmly, "As I've tried to make clear, I'm interested only in the work I came here to do. I have no intention of getting in your way, and I hope that you'll not get in mine."

"You just remember what I said," Corbett cautioned her.

"Oh, I'm sure it will be a long time before I forget our meeting," Jessie told him. "And I'm equally sure that we'll manage to get along. Now, I don't want to keep you from the work that you've been telling me keeps you so busy. I'll bid you good day, Mr. Corbett."

Without giving the Indian agent time to reply, Jessie wheeled around and left the office. She stood outside the door for a moment, looking around the cavernous structure. It was as crowded and as busy as it had been when she entered. The buzzing of many conversations in the lines of waiting Indians, and the extra noises coming from those waiting in clusters along the walls, seemed even louder than it had been when she first entered.

Jessie was looking around to find the nearest door leading outside when voices rising in angry tones from the end of the long counter nearest her drew her attention. As Jessie turned to find the source, it occurred to her that she might have stumbled onto an argument which would open a path to discovering something connected with her mission.

She started toward the sounds, moving carefully and slowly to avoid attracting attention to herself. Even before she'd taken a few steps she saw that the argument was between a blanket-draped Indian and the clerk behind the long counter. She edged closer in order to hear clearly what they were saying.

"You folks just have got to understand that we ain't got all that much beef to give out," the clerk was explaining.

"Paper say we get all one back-leg," the Indian said. "We need for people so much beef. Ribs not got same meat."

"That's something I can't help," the clerk went on. "All I can give out is what's on this list."

"List wrong," the man insisted. "Not say back-leg same like one I got. You give me back-leg."

"Like I keep telling you, we ain't got no hind-quarters." Now the clerk was raising his voice. He went on, "What you better do is take what you got and go over to the allotment table yonder. Tell 'em what you told me, maybe they'll give you another stand of ribs. That'd just about add up to how much meat you'd get from a haunch."

While the argument between the Indian and the clerk was seesawing back and forth, the Indians waiting in line had been growing more and more restless. The man standing behind the one who claimed he'd been shorted pushed the complaining Indian aside.

"You give him back-leg, I get back-leg too," he told the clerk, raising his voice to be heard above the growing murmurs from the Indians waiting behind him.

"Now, listen to me, damn it!" the ration clerk exclaimed. He slapped a hand on the counter. The banging sound made when his palm struck the wood of the countertop cut above the buzz of voices. The murmurs from the Indians who'd been crowding up died away. The clerk went on, "A steer ain't got but two hind legs, and all of you know that! Somebody's got to take the ribs and the little front legs!"

These were the last words that Jessie heard clearly, for the din in the big room was mounting in ripples as word of the dispute spread to the crowded Indians who'd been standing in the other ration lines. A few of the men raised their voices in shouts, and within a few seconds their yells were coming from all sides as the waiting Indians joined in what Jessie took to be a spontaneous protest of the rationing system. Then two shots cut through the din and the calls subsided.

Jessie swiveled, looking for the source of the shots. She saw Rafe Corbett standing in front of his office door, his revolver dangling from his hand. Only a handful of the protesters were yelling now and the Indian agent holstered his gun.

"Stop this ruckus!" he shouted. "You don't shut it off, I call the bluecoats!"

A few more scattered shouts rose when Corbett ended his threat, but they died away quickly and only the chatter of a few isolated voices broke the silence that had settled inside the big building. The lines began to re-form. Corbett watched for a moment, then turned and went back into his office.

Jessie watched for a moment while the Indians slowly re-formed their lines in front of the counter. Then she picked her way through the clusters of Indians who had regrouped along the walls and went to rejoin Ki. He was squatting down beside the wagon, watching the Indian encampment. She settled beside him.

"Did you learn anything useful from your visit?" he asked.

"Yes and no," she replied. "I'll tell you more later, but I know this much right now. The Indian Bureau's even more corrupt here than General Nesbitt seems to realize."

"We suspected that from the first," Ki nodded. "So it's not any real surprise."

"There's a lot of dissatisfaction over the rationing system," Jessie went on. "We've already gotten a hint of that. My guess is that whoever's running it is stealing the choicer cuts from the steers they butcher for the Indians' rations."

"I wouldn't call that a surprise," Ki told her.

"Of course not. We can work on it later after we've found out how the stealing's being done. And I have a very strong hunch that there's some wholesale theft involving the food vouchers the Indian Bureau has put in."

"I'd say that your visit was very productive, Jessie, if you've found out all that in such a short time."

"Oh, that's not all," she went on. "But from the impression I got while I was talking to the head agent and listening to the Indians, I'm sure we'll be spending a longer time here than we'd anticipated. I think our first job's going to be finding some place where we can be at least partly comfortable."

"We didn't see anything even remotely like a town, or even a squatter settlement on the way here," Ki said. "Usually, where an army fort's been occupied for any length of time, a few settlers begin a town somewhere nearby."

"Even if we didn't see any sign of one, there may be some sort of settlement upriver from the fort, here," Jessie suggested. "Remember, when we saw the Indian tepees and the fort buildings we turned downriver."

"There just might be at that," Ki agreed. "And if I was settling on a stream close to an army fort, I'd want to be upstream from the fort, where I could be sure the water was clean."

"I wasn't thinking of trails or roads," Jessie told him. "Though it might be handy to know a little about them. But the horses have had a good rest and we're not pressed for time, Ki. Let's go do a little scouting."

"Even if we were just guessing, we guessed right," Jessie said. She gestured toward the dark, straight horizontal lines that had appeared suddenly a few minutes after they started up the low ridge the wagon was now mounting. "Those lines are rooftops, or I'm missing my guess."

"There's no guesswork involved," Ki said. "They're houses, all right, even if there aren't many of them."

"Houses close together that way mean a town, and a town means a store of some kind. We just happened to miss it when we were heading for the fort. If we'd taken the other fork on that trail where it split, we'd've come to the town before we reached Fort Supply. But it's strange that it doesn't show on our map."

"I'd imagine some careless mapmaker just happened to leave it off," Jessie suggested. "Now that we can see a bit more, I'd guess there are only a dozen or so houses."

"If there are that many," Ki agreed. "But we'll know for sure after we top this rise."

They sat in silence as the wagon moved along. Each yard gained gave them a more complete view of the settlement. Jessie's guess that the town had only a few more than a dozen houses proved to be very nearly correct, for as they topped the rise and could get a clear view of the tiny huddle of dwellings on the downslope they counted eleven houses. Five of them huddled closely together along the road; the remainder were scattered on the downslope. Between the houses they could see the weathered remains of foundations where at an earlier time other houses had stood.

"There certainly isn't much left of the town," Jessie remarked as the team started down the gentle slope.

Ki was pulling on the brake to keep the wagon from rolling downslope onto the horses. After he'd found the balance point where brakes and horsepower were equalized, he turned to Jessie and replied, "It's easy to guess what happened. A lot of the western forts were closed down when the war ended. It's possible that Fort Supply was one of them, and people moved away."

"I hope there'll be a store of some kind here," Jessie said. "We're going to have to buy food, and after my little run-in with that Indian agent, I don't think we'd be welcomed at the agency's commissary."

"That could be embarassing," Ki nodded. "Because I have a feeling that Rafe Corbett would order the agency's commissary not to sell us anything, and the closest place where we found to buy supplies on the way here would be a two-day haul each way."

They'd been moving steadily while they talked, and now the wagon was almost abreast of the first house in the ghostly half-abandoned town. There was no one visible around it, and the ground in front of the narrow porch and on all sides of the dwelling was barren.

"There's certainly no reason to stop here," Ki said. "The place looks totally deserted, Jessie."

"Not quite." Jessie gestured ahead as she spoke. "That place up ahead seems to be occupied."

Ahead, Ki saw the house to which Jessie had pointed. It stood a bit away from the others along the trail, just becoming visible beyond a lazy curve of the road. Even at a distance they could see that the house bore a battered tin sign above its doorstep. A wagon loaded with gleaming yellow freshly sawed lumber stood in front of the house, its team tethered to the hitch rail. As the team pulling their wagon reached the turn in the curving road, the lettering on the sign above the house door became visible. It read STORE.

"Look, Ki!" Jessie exclaimed. "A store! And that wagon's team is still hitched, so that means it must still be in business. That store's bound to have airtights and things like flour and sugar and dry beans. And it's not all that far from Fort Supply. Now we don't have to worry about having to depend on the Indian Bureau's commissary. We can just ride up and get our supplies here."

"It's not any further from here to the fort than it is to the railroad whistle-stop at the Circle Star," Ki agreed. "And I have a feeling that it might be to our advantage not to be too near Fort Supply."

"Then let's stop here and find out what the store's like," Jessie suggested. "It'll give the horses a breather."

They reached the hitch rail and dismounted. Knotting the reins of the team, they started toward the door of the house. Before they reached the first step, Jessie stopped short and turned to look at the lumber-laden wagon. She studied its load for a moment—stacks of wide, gleaming, freshly milled pine boards.

"I've got an idea, Ki," she announced. "We're far enough away from the fort in this place here to have breathing space, and still be close enough to do the job we've been sent to handle. Suppose I buy that load of lumber and we'll put up a little shack, only a floor and roof to start with, to keep the rain off of us when one of those prairie downpours comes along. Don't you think that's a good idea?"

★

Chapter 8

For a moment Ki stared at Jessie. At last he said, "You've really surprised me this time. Building a house here is the last thing I'd've expected you to suggest."

"If you think about it for a minute, I'm sure you'll agree it's a practical idea. We certainly ought to know enough to build one, Ki. Goodness knows, we've spent enough time supervising and watching the carpenters who've put up new stables and barns on the Circle Star."

"You always seem to have a reason for whatever you're planning to do, Jessie. Suppose you tell me why you think it's such a good idea to have a place up here. Wouldn't it be too far from the fort to be useful?"

"In my luggage I've got the Leitz binoculars Alex gave me, Ki," Jessie replied. "With them we can watch Fort Supply as well as the Indian camp without calling attention to ourselves."

"That does make sense," Ki nodded. "When we get too close to the Indians they seem to be a bit uneasy."

"Yes, I've noticed how they keep looking at us like they wish we'd go away," she answered. "If we keep our distance most of the time and just go into the Indian camps occasionally, it might make our job easier. And when the weather's bad we'd be a lot less exposed. Summer's not going to last forever, and we don't know how long we're going to be here in the Indian Nation."

"I'll have to agree those are pretty good reasons," Ki told her. "But we'd have to get Corbett's permission if we built on Indian Agency land. That might be a real job, and even if he approved it, finding a location for a house wouldn't be easy with all those Indian tepees around the fort."

"But think how much easier it would be for us to keep an eye on things if we had a place where we could see the whole valley."

"There's no question about that, Jessie. But to do that, we'd have to be on high ground, and there really isn't any except for the little ridge on the northwest where that creek runs down to the river."

"Exactly," Jessie agreed. "And that's the only direction the Indians haven't taken over for their camp. They've picked the level ground beyond the fort."

"We've got the wagon, of course," Ki pointed out. "We could just pull it up close to the tepees. We've still got the canvas cover tucked away in the load, and it'd be easy to cut some green tree limbs and bend them into arches to support it. Then we could make enough space inside for our bedrolls."

Jessie shook her head. "I'm afraid that wouldn't be a good idea. If we camp too close to the Indians they're likely to think we were sent by the Indian Bureau or the army to spy on them—instead of being sent by the army to spy on the Indian Bureau."

Ki nodded and smiled, then said, "And you'll have to agree that they have a pretty good good reason to think that."

"We both know the Indians aren't fools, Ki."

"Of course we do, Jessie," he agreed. "It's impossible for them not to know that the Indian Bureau's stealing their food, and I'm sure they're not going to stand for it too long. What you saw and heard when you were in the bureau's headquarters can't be just one incident of its kind."

"What it all comes down to," Jessie went on thoughtfully, "is that we've got to be close enough to make watching the fort easy, but far enough away to keep both the Indian Bureau people and the Indians from getting ideas about us that'd stir them up."

"That might be easier said than done," Ki told her. "But I'll agree that we do need somewhere to settle down in."

"What we need is a place where we can watch the Indian Bureau and the Indians for signs of trouble," Jessie said. "A burst of activity, soldiers arriving— things of that sort. We need a source to get information from inside the bureau, of course, but it's going to take some time to develop that."

"And probably a bit longer to find out what's taking place among the Indians," Ki said. "But they seem to accept me as a sort of distant cousin, so that's what I'll work on."

"It's just occurred to me, Ki, that we can surely find a spot in that high ground we've just ridden over," Jessie went on. "And if this store has any kind of stock, we wouldn't have to worry about losing time, having to travel a day or two for a supply of food."

"Everything you've said makes sense," Ki nodded. "And I suppose that whoever owns that load of lumber is inside the store, so let's go in and see what we can do."

Jessie and Ki walked over to the house that bore the sign STORE. The outer screen door was closed, but the wooden door behind it was wide open and through the screen's mesh they could see a man standing behind a counter that spanned the room beyond. He nodded as they entered.

"Howdy, folks," he greeted them. "Something I can do for you today?"

"I'm sure there is," Jessie replied. "We'll be buying some food while we're here, but first I'd like to find out about that wagonload of lumber at the hitching post."

"Why, it ain't mine, ma'am," the storekeeper replied. "The teamsters just stopped to—" he halted abruptly and was silent for a moment before continuing, "to rest a little bit."

"I suppose they'll be coming back to their wagon pretty soon, won't they?" Ki asked.

"Oh, sure," the merchant nodded. "They're just— well, they ain't very far away."

"We'll wait for them, then," Jessie said. "And we're getting a bit short on food, so while we're waiting we can pick out the things we need."

"Trade's always welcome," the storekeeper told her. "Now, I don't have garden truck, since everybody but me and—" he stopped short. "Since the army up and moved away everybody else when they were clearing things out for the redskins, and this place begun to be called the Indian Nation."

"I see," Jessie replied. "But they let you stay?"

"Well, you see, they didn't clear out the panhandle— that little chunk that's between Texas and Kansas. They figured the folks there needed a store close by. But that ain't here nor there. Is there anything special I can get for you, ma'am?"

"I suppose you have some airtights?" Jessie asked.

"Oh, sure. I got the best, right out of the Underwood and Prescott plant back East. Green peas and beans and tomatoes and peaches and plums. I even got a few of them new airtights with beans and chunks of pork in 'em. And I got crackers and all like that. You just take your time and look around and tell me what you fancy. If you find something, just call me. My name's Ecks Kokely. You show me what you want, I'll get it all together for you and tote it out to your wagon."

As though the word 'wagon' had been a cue, a burst of laughter sounded outside, then the door was pulled open and two men pushed into the store. Jessie and Ki turned to look. Both men were in shirtsleeves, but both carried the sort of heavy canvas coats worn by teamsters. Their laughing died away when they saw Jessie and Ki.

"Hey, Pat!" one of them said. "Ain't she a real fine piece! Maybe we left that kip too quick!"

"I'd say you're right," his companion answered. "But I've had all I need right now. But on the way back we'll sure—"

"Shut up, you fools!" Kokely snapped angrily. "This lady's a customer!"

Abruptly the men stopped laughing, their faces showing their embarrassment. Then one of them said, "Ma'am, I'm sorry we stepped outa line. You see—"

"Don't make things any worse!" the storekeeper went on. "Unless you've got to buy something to eat, get on back out to your wagon and start moving on to Fort Supply!"

"Wait just a moment, Mr. Kokely," Jessie broke in. "I'm sure you must be talking about that wagonload of lumber outside, since it's the only wagon around besides the one Ki and I are traveling in. Do I understand that it belongs to these men?"

"It does," Kokely replied. "And—well, I didn't mention it before, when we were talking about everybody moving away from here. I was a little bit bothered about saying anything because it's—" He stopped, looking from Jessie to Ki, the perplexed frown on his face speaking for itself.

"Don't feel embarrassed on my account," Jessie said quickly. "From what I've just heard, I'm sure what you're talking about must be a brothel."

"It is, ma'am," the storekeeper replied. Jessie's words seemed to have released the restraint he'd been exercising. He went on, "When the army was clearing out everybody around here, getting ready for the Indians to come in, they let the girls stay right where they was. There's only two of 'em, anyways."

"I see," Jessie replied. "Now, if you'll excuse me, I need to talk to these men. Perhaps—"

Ki broke in. "I hate to interrupt you, Jessie, but I don't see any reason for me to join you, and it'll save time if I start picking out what we need. Just call if you want me for something."

With a nod, Jessie turned back to the teamsters. She said, "That looks like very good lumber on your wagon. I suppose you're starting out to sell it?"

"Well, not exactly, ma'am," the man called Pat replied. "It ain't exactly sold, but it's spoke for. Me and Sam was on our way to Fort Supply to deliver it."

"Did the Indian Bureau order those boards on your wagon?" Ki asked.

Pat frowned as he answered, "I ain't real sure whether the boss man there at the fort ordered 'em for the gov'mint or for hisself. He didn't write out no order, just told us about what he wanted."

"Then you don't have a closed deal," Jessie said thoughtfully. "If it was a government order you'd have it in writing."

"Well, I take an order to be an order, ma'am. That fellow at Fort Supply wouldn't't've told us to bring him them boards if he didn't aim to pay us for 'em."

"But don't you see?" she persisted. "All that you're really doing is hauling a load of lumber to Fort Supply without being sure you'll get paid for it."

"Well, ma'am, I know a deal ain't closed till money changes hands, but I reckon we'll get our money, even if we might have to wait around for it a day or so."

"And waste your time," she reminded them. "Since you don't have a government requisition, and haven't been paid, and can't even be sure you'll ever be paid, I might be able to save you a lot of time and trouble."

"How's that, ma'am?" one of the men asked.

"Suppose I buy those boards myself," Jessie replied. "I'll take them off your hands for a bit more than you've been offered. How much is in your load and what were you going to charge the man who ordered them?"

Neither of the men spoke for a moment. They just looked at one another and exchanged nods. Then Sam said, "We got a hundred one-by-twelves and twenty two-by-fours, ma'am, all twelve-foot lengths. He said he'd pay us a dime a running foot."

Jessie had handled enough deals in stock exchanges and cattle markets to be quick at mental arithmetic. Almost before Sam had finished speaking, she said, "That would be a hundred twenty dollars. I'll give you a hundred forty, gold coin, spot cash when you've unloaded them."

Before his partner could reply, Sam asked, "You mean we can just unload right here?"

"Not here, but just a little distance away, between here and the fort," Jessie said. She turned to Ki and asked, "Do you remember the high spot where the creek's cut through that bluff, Ki?"

"Of course," he nodded. "By the rock outcrop where we had to ford the creek and stopped to look back. Isn't that the place you have in mind, Jessie?"

"That's it," she nodded. Turning to the teamsters, she asked, "Do we have a deal?"

"Well, now, we was looking for—"

"A better offer?" Jessie broke in to ask. She shook her head. "I'm offering a better price than you've been expecting to get, and you'll cut your trip short by a full day, counting the time you'd spend going on to Fort Supply and losing time while you unloaded, then coming back. And right this minute, you're still not sure your load's sold."

"Sounds to me like the lady's making sense," Pat told his partner. "And that fellow at the fort, he's not looking for us today or tomorrow, we can go get another load for him."

"There's one thing more," Ki broke in. "Do you have nails in your load?"

Before either of the teamsters could reply, Ecks Kokely said, "I got all kinds of nails, kegs of 'em, in my back room. Make you a good price too."

"That settles it, then," Jessie said. She turned back to the teamsters. "We've got a deal, haven't we? I'm prepared to pay you spot cash when that lumber's unloaded, a few miles down the road."

"We sure have got a deal," Sam replied without waiting for his partner's agreement. "You just show us where you want 'em."

Jessie turned to Ki and said, "Suppose I ride on with these men in their wagon, Ki. I'll show them where we want the lumber stacked. You pick out the nails we'll need."

"While I'm buying things, I'd better get some air-tights too," Ki suggested. "We're beginning to run low on food."

"Then get what we need to tide us over," Jessie said. "We'll want to stay here and build our cabin. It's not too late to start today. We'll see how much we can get done before dark."

Crouching down around the waning coals of their break-fast fire, Jessie and Ki looked at what they'd been able to accomplish during the short time they'd been able to spend working before darkness fell the day before.

"It really doesn't look like too much, does it?" Jessie asked.

"No, but tonight will tell another story," Ki replied.

"We had to think about water first, of course," Jessie went on. "And that little spring is a real lifesaver."

Ki had discovered the small trickling spring near the top of the rise while they were choosing the best place to build their cabin. Though its rivulet of clear water running into the river was thin and shallow, any work on the cabin had been postponed. They'd worked until dark digging a dishpan-sized catchbasin and lining it with rocks, and the little excavation full of clear sparkling water had been their early-morning reward.

Jessie gestured toward the disturbed patches of earth where they'd begun to level the slanting ground before finding the spring. She said, "We won't have much shovel work to do, Ki. Just a little digging and a few big rocks are all that's going to be needed for a foundation."

"Yes, the slant in the ground's so gentle in that place we picked that I can do all the shovel work in a couple of hours," he replied. "And the only big rocks we'll have to worry about are those we need at the corners. If we can't find any loose ones that are big enough, I'll cut some two-by-fours and spike them together to make the four corner blocks we'll need."

For the next few hours while the sun climbed toward midday, Jessie and Ki worked in companionable silence. The spot they'd picked for their impromptu shelter was the best place offered on the gently rising slope that stretched away from the trail.

They'd agreed on the location immediately, once they'd made sure that the orientation of the cabin allowed for the door to be placed where it provided a clear vista that took in the Indian Agency headquarters on the flat prairie that stretched to the horizon. The slant in the ground was so gentle that it required little leveling other than that needed at each corner, and the shovel work was completed by noon.

"We've put in a good morning's work," Jessie commented, looking at the two-by-fours they were doubling and nailing together to be spliced into foundation

108

sills. "But it looks like we haven't really made much progress."

"We'll get a lot done this afternoon," Ki replied. He went on, "Building the kind of little shanty we need isn't going to be a big job, if we just ignore such things as cracks between the boards in the wall, a doorway without a door, and windows with no glass to put in them."

"To say nothing of a dirt floor and no fireplace or chimney, and a roof without shingles and cracks between the boards in the walls," Jessie added with a smile. "But anything's better than no shelter at all, Ki. And I'm certainly not complaining."

"We ought to be able to get at least two of the walls up before dark," Ki went on without turning from his study of the ground where the freshly turned dirt from the shallow rectangle they'd shoveled lay ready to receive the foundation stringers. "And we can probably get the other two walls and most of the roof finished by this time tomorrow."

"We don't have to be in any hurry," Jessie told him. "But the sooner we can settle in and start on the job we really came here to do, the better I'll like it."

"Well, we did it, Ki, even if it shows that we aren't very good carpenters," Jessie said.

She and Ki were standing on the gentle slope looking at the boards of the completed cabin shining yellow-gold in the late morning sunlight.

"As rough as it is, it doesn't look as bad as I was afraid it would," Ki agreed. "Of course, we don't have a stove or any furniture, but it'll shelter us from the weather and be a place where we can rest and sleep."

"Now all we have to do is unload the wagon and put things to order in the cabin," Jessie went on. "After we've finished unloading we'll saddle the horses and ride down to the Indian Agency. I'm anxious to get started on the job General Nesbitt asked us to do."

"I'll begin the unloading," Ki volunteered. "You stay in the cabin and tell me where you'd like things put."

"That won't be much of a problem, traveling light the way we are. But it'll still take an hour or more to get the job done."

They began working, unloading the boxes and parcels from the wagon bed and arranging them inside the small cabin. They stopped only long enough to make a quick pickup lunch of summer sausage and crackers before going back to their job. Jessie had just deposited a box on the cabin floor and was stepping through the doorless doorway when she glimpsed the horsemen riding up the narrow strip of road from the fort.

"Ki!" she called. "We're going to have visitors."

"From the Indian Agency, I suppose?" he asked.

"Of course. Two men. I got just a glimpse of them before they started up the rise and got behind that rock shoulder over yonder, but I'm pretty sure one of them was Rafe Corbett."

Ki deposited the box he was carrying in the middle of the cabin floor and stepped to the door to join Jessie. He glanced down the trail, but the approaching horsemen had not yet rounded the high rock shoulder that hid the bend in the road.

"He's probably just noticed our cabin and is coming to find out about it," Jessie suggested.

"I imagine you're right," Ki agreed. "And he may have the right to ask us. We're not at all certain about the point where the Indian Bureau's boundary begins.

It could take in more land or less than the fort did."

"Well, we'll know soon enough," Jessie went on as the pair of horsemen came in sight where the trail straightened out. "That's Corbett on the roan, I've never seen the man on the dapple before."

"They're close enough now for me to understand why you got such a bad impression of him when you visited him," Ki told Jessie as the pair of riders drew closer. "He does look more like a thug than I'd imagined."

"Just don't forget that I'm Jessie Star now," she said, dropping her voice as the two men reached the narrow strip of land that stretched between the road and the cabin.

"I won't," Ki promised, dropping his voice as the riders reined in and dismounted.

"Well, well!" Corbett exclaimed as he and his companion started up the low, easy slope. "I figured you'd gone back to where you belong, to write another kind of book, about something besides Indians, Miss—Miss Jessie Star—as I remember."

"I thought I made it clear when we were talking that I had no intention of giving up my idea," Jessie said cooly. "Even if you did try to discourage me."

"So you did," Corbett nodded. "But you didn't say you was going to try to be a squatter on the reservation. And you didn't come ask me if you could put up a house—if you can call it that. So I've got some real bad news for you, Miss Star. Nobody puts up a house here without my say-so. If you got any goods in there that you want to keep, you better get 'em out in a hurry, because we've come to burn your little shack down, plumb to the ground."

★

Chapter 9

Though Corbett's words sent a burst of anger through her, Jessie did not allow her expression to change. She locked her eyes with his, and Corbett accepted her unspoken challenge. They stared silently at one another while the tension between them grew. It was Corbett who moved his head first and broke the invisible chain that had bound them together. When the Indian agent finally spoke, his voice was full of rancor.

"Well, Miss Star," he said. "I've given you fair warning. If you and your servant have got anything worth saving out of all the truck scattered around in here, I'll hold up firing the place till you've carried whatever you want to save outside."

"I don't intend to see any of our belongings burned!" Jessie said emphatically. "And that includes this cabin!"

"Being stubborn won't get you anywheres," Corbett snapped. "And you better start clearing out, because

I've used up all my patience. But my offer's still good, and I'll give you just one more chance. As soon as Hawkins can scrape up some kindling wood and pile it in the middle of the floor there, I'm going to touch a match to it."

"I'd suggest that you wait long enough for me to get a letter out of my portmanteau, Mr. Corbett," Jessie told him. "You may want to change your plans after you read it."

"I can't see what a letter you've been carrying around has anything to do with this," Corbett frowned. "But get it out. I'll wait long enough to look at it before I touch a match to this place you've put up."

Jessie stepped over to where her portmanteau rested in one corner of the little room and took out the "bearer" letter given her at the Circle Star by General Nesbitt. Unfolding it as she returned to Corbett, she handed it to him. As the Indian agent scanned the brief missive his jaw dropped and his eyebrows started upward. When he saw the signature, his jaws were fully agape and his eyes had opened so wide that they appeared to be bulging from their sockets. He swallowed hard and the effort sent his features back to normal. He read the letter a second time, then turned to Jessie.

"Seems like you've got some friends in high places, Miss Star," he said. "How come you didn't trot this out and show it to me when you come visiting my office?"

"One reason is that I didn't have it with me," Jessie replied. "Perhaps I'd have mentioned having it if your discourteous manner hadn't been so irritating. However, now that you've seen the letter I hope that you realize I'm serious about staying here to gather material for the book I propose to write."

114

"Well, I reckon that's your privilege, Miss Star," Corbett said slowly. "Only I don't see what in—" Stopping short, he shook his head before going on. "I didn't know the president was so much concerned about the redskins, but I don't happen to be fool enough to cut off my nose to spite my face. Just don't you look for me to change my mind about you not having any business coming here."

"I think you've made that quite clear," Jessie told him. "But it would make me feel a great deal better if you assure me that there won't be any more incidents such as this one."

"Oh, I'll see to that, all right," he nodded. "You go ahead and talk to the Indians all you want, but don't ever forget that I'm head of the Indian Agency, and I'll expect you to stay out of my way."

"I haven't any intention to spend my time in your office," Jessie assured him. "My interest is in the Indians."

Corbett nodded. He turned to his companion and gestured toward the door. Neither Jessie nor Ki spoke until the two men had mounted and started away. Then Jessie turned to Ki.

"I think we won, but I'm not sure, Ki," she said.

"That's about the way I feel," Ki told her. "But I'd say you came out ahead."

"Let's leave it at that and get busy," Jessie went on. "Now that we've settled in, we can really get started."

"Yes, because it's possible that this will turn out to be just our starting point," Ki said. "We might find it necessary to do some more traveling."

"You're thinking now about what General Nesbitt said, that the Ghost Dance unrest started among the

Sioux up in Dakota Territory?"

Ki nodded. "And how the army's concerned about it spreading to the other Indian tribes further North. But if it's moving North, it's certain to come South too. While we were listening to General Nesbitt, I got a somewhat strange feeling that he was trying to describe a situation he wasn't really familiar with."

Jessie nodded as she said, "I got the same impression myself, Ki. Then, after he'd already started back to his headquarters, it occurred to me that he was trying to indicate that he was letting us make our own decisions about where to go and what to look for."

"It could've been that, of course," Ki agreed.

"What I wondered about most is why he didn't send us right on to Dakota Territory, if that's where the trouble is," she went on. "But after I'd thought things over, I decided that what he might've intended was for us to start here and get acquainted with the problems first."

"Getting our feet wet by wading in, not jumping off the bank and into the river before we can swim?"

"Something like that," Jessie nodded. "The only thing he was specific about was that the general staff didn't know as much as they felt they should."

"That's very likely," Ki agreed. "And I don't suppose they could've sent us to a better place. Even from the little we've seen so far, just about every Indian tribe in the country seems to be represented here, including the Sioux."

"Yes, they're the ones we need to think about first. And since that seems to be the case, we'd better get busy," Jessie went on. "Let's go, Ki. I don't think Rafe Corbett's going to bother us again, and our cabin will be safe."

"I'm not worrying about Corbett giving us any more trouble," Ki smiled. "Your credentials set him back on his heels pretty thoroughly."

"So I noticed," Jessie agreed. "So let's ride down to Fort Supply and see if we can find some friendly Indians who'll talk with us."

"If that's what you wish, of course. Get your weapons and I'll get my *shuriken* and we'll go at once," Ki nodded.

"There's not much we can do except to study the lay of the land a bit more," Jessie said. "But I'm very interested in finding out if the Northern Sioux plan to start teaching the Ghost Dance here in the Indian Nation."

"Or if they already have," Ki suggested as he and Jessie left the cabin and started for their horses.

"Just look at all those Indians around the agency building, Ki!" Jessie exclaimed as they rounded the last curve in the winding trail and passed the high bluff that had hidden the lower ground of the huge circular valley. "Something's certainly happening there."

She gestured toward the big, rambling structure that dominated the shallow bowl-shaped valley stretching out just below them. The wide area of ground surrounding the Indian Agency building had been much less crowded when they'd ridden out only three days earlier. Now it was completely covered with clusters of Indians and their sheltering tepees. Many of the Indians had simply spread a blanket on the grass to lounge on, and some of the groups were squatting down or stretched out on the grass.

Some of the Indians did not seem to have found space in which to settle. Singly and in groups of two or three they wandered from one cluster to another, stopping to exchange a few words, perhaps just to wave a hand or to strike palms in wordless greetings. In the near distance, conical tops of tepees and the black circles of burned wood marked camping spaces. These and the big adobe building itself were unchanged from the short inspection given them by Jessie and Ki when they'd first arrived at Fort Supply.

Outnumbering the more distant loungers by many dozens was the group that had congregated in front of the door of the Indian Agency. These were not lounging, but formed compact knots of as few as three or four and as many as eight or ten. Jessie and Ki could not hear what the Indians were saying, or understand the arm-wavings and crossings of fingers or brushings of their hands in sign language—a means of communication which was as commonplace as spoken words.

"I can't understand why it didn't occur to us before, Ki," Jessie said after they'd ridden a short distance farther. "But look at the door where the crowd's thickest. I just got a glimpse of an Indian woman carrying a big towsack over her shoulder. It was empty, but from the way she was hurrying toward the agency, she must've been on her way to get it filled. This must be one of the days when the Indians draw their government rations."

"Of course," Ki nodded. "That hadn't occurred to me, either. But I'm sure it's the explanation."

"I'm surprised to see such a crowd, though," Jessie went on. "I suppose we didn't cover enough ground when we took our little ride the other day. It didn't seem to me that there was such a large number of Indians here."

"That was my impression, too," he agreed. "But it's just occurred to me that with all those Indians gathered up around the agency building, this might be a good time to ask some of them about finding a few Northern Sioux. Certainly there'll be some here, in a group of this size."

"It wouldn't surprise me if you're right," Jessie replied. "And I think it's pretty apparent that there've been a lot come here after we did. With all the new arrivals, we shouldn't have any trouble finding one or two who'll talk to us, especially if we offer to pay him."

They'd reached the end of the downslope now and were getting close to the agency building. There were only a few scattered Indians in the narrow stretch of ground that remained between them and the fringes of the crowd. Jessie was looking for the best course to take in circling the congested area just ahead when a scattering of loud angry shouts arose from the direction of the agency building.

Jessie and Ki both turned their heads to look in the direction of the noise, but even in their saddles with their eyes well above the crowd they could see nothing but a confused mass of bobbing heads and upraised arms at the door of the Indian Agency headquarters. Reining in, Jessie stood up in her stirrups and Ki quickly followed her example.

Now they could see that three Indians who'd just come out of the agency were in the center of a small group of a dozen or so who were bending over to look at something on the ground. They could not tell what was drawing the men's attention, for by now a compact group had formed around them. There was a great deal of head-bobbing among the newest arrivals, who in the space of only a few instants had engulfed the original dozen.

119

"Something's about to happen," Jessie said to Ki. "But it's not our affair. Let's stay here and watch."

"It might be a good idea to get closer before we stop," Ki suggested. "I just got a glimpse of Rafe Corbett coming out the door. He was carrying a rifle, and from our experience, Jessie, we've certainly found out that where he goes trouble is pretty sure to follow."

"Even if there's trouble, it needn't concern us," Jessie said, frowning. "But after the way he tried to treat us up in our cabin, I have no use for him." She paused for a moment, then added, "But it is a good idea to get closer, where we can hear what's being said. In a few minutes there's going to be such a crowd around Corbett that even from our saddles we might not be able to see a great deal."

Jessie was toeing her horse ahead before she'd stopped speaking. Ki wasted no time in following her. They kept their eyes on Corbett as they drew closer to the agency building. He was already half-hidden by the Indians who were closing around him, but they could still get occasional glimpses of him.

Corbett was still standing just outside the agency building's door, his rifle cradled in a crooked elbow, looking at the crowd that was forming around the three sack-toting Indians a few yards away. As Jessie and Ki drew closer, keeping their horses at a walk, they could hear bursts of angry voices but could not yet distinguish the words being spoken. The Indians who were still moving toward the building dodged and swerved to avoid them and their horses.

A fresh burst of strident voices, those of several men, each one trying to drown out the others, sounded from the midst of the milling throng that had now spread along the wall of the building. Jessie and Ki reined in until, from the high vantage point of their saddles, they were near enough to the center of the forming crowd to see Corbett and the Indian men standing with him. They were also able to catch a word or two, but both Corbett and the Indians were speaking in one of the tribal tongues.

"I wish we knew what they were saying!" Jessie said in a half-whisper to Ki. "But watching Rafe Corbett's face, I gather that he's as much at sea as we are."

Corbett proved the truth of Jessie's words by waving his arms and bringing the palm of his hands up to cover his mouth. He repeated the gesture before the Indians crowding around him fell silent. Then he pointed to the door from which he'd originally emerged, then brought his fingers together and worked fingers and thumb in a ducks-bill movement.

One of the Indians in the little bunch clustered around Corbett nodded and gestured to those between the Indian agent and the door to stand aside. Corbett stepped to the door. He opened it only wide enough to stick his head in and shout a word or two. A moment later he stepped aside as the door opened and one of the agency men came out.

By this time Jessie and Ki had reached the edge of the little group of Indians surrounding Corbett. They stopped just in time to hear the agency clerk address the Indians in what was obviously their own language. The Indian who had assumed command of his fellow tribesmen surprised them when he replied in very precise English, speaking slowly as though he were talking to a child.

"I will talk to the chief man in your tongue," he told the newcomer. "You put my words into the Dakota

121

tongue, which is the one all my people speak. Do you know it well?"

When the clerk replied, it was in a language which neither Jessie nor Ki understood, but the Indians' spokesman nodded.

"You speak our language truly," he said. "That is a good thing. We must be sure there is no misunderstanding between us."

His features showing his bewilderment, the agency man looked questioningly at Corbett, who nodded with a deepening of the scowl that still twisted his face.

"Tell the men of my people to open the parcel," the Indian leader instructed the agency clerk.

Addressing the three men standing beside their gunny sack bundles, the clerk looked at the Indian leader, who nodded as much to the Indians as to the clerk. Bending over their bundles, the Indians fumbled the wrappings away. Small stacks of steer ribs were revealed. The meat on the ribs was almost black and the strips of fatty tallow tissue between them oozed a dribble of brownish, gummy semiliquid.

Almost at the moment the wrappings had been removed, a nauseating odor began assaulting the nostrils of the onlookers. Jessie and Ki had to fight to keep from gagging as the smell reached them. Forcing themselves to ignore the stench they stared at the oozing slabs of meat.

"Why, that meat's rotten, Ki!" Jessie whispered. "Not even a hungry coyote would eat it! You can see just how bad it is at a glance! Is that what the Indian Bureau's been giving these Indians?"

"You'd have to ask Corbett that question," Ki replied in the same low whisper. "But I strongly suspect that it is."

"No wonder the Indians are restless!" Jessie said. "Why, I wouldn't give meat like that to a coyote, much less—" She broke off when the chief spoke again.

"Others of our people have spoken of this to me," he said, his black eyes fixed on Corbett. "We of the Sioux, the Dakota and Lakota and Nakota have made a peace with your people and given up lands that were ours because you promised us good lands and food in return. We have kept our promises to you. But now you cheat us."

"That ain't my fault!" Corbett protested. "I don't buy the meat, there's men back in Washington that contracts to buy it, and all I can do is give you what they send me!"

"Then tell these men you speak of that we will not be cheated anymore!" the Sioux chief said. "I know you have the talking wires that carry words fast. Go now and tell them there will be no more cheating! Tell them that if we do not have good meat in three days we will have war!"

Corbett did not answer, and in the silence that held while the chief waited for a reply Jessie whispered to Ki, "After what we've just seen, I'd be tempted to overlook the way Corbett treated us and give the Indians a couple of good steers from the Circle Star herds, Ki. But it's too far from here to make that possible."

"It's not your responsibility, either. And there isn't any railroad line that can get meat or a live steer here even from the Fort Worth stockyards in less than a week."

"Let's see how Corbett solves his problem," Jessie said. "He can't wait much longer to give some sort of answer."

Almost as though Jessie's words had been a cue, Corbett began waving his arms above his head and shouting.

"Listen to me!" he called at the top of his voice, "You people in front pass the word along to the ones in back of you that might not hear or understand what I'm about to say! We'll have some fresh meat sent here as soon as I can send a telegram! It'll take some time for it to get here, but so as to tide you over, I'm having some airtights and other stuff brought up from the agency warehouse! Just wait a little while and we'll have food to give you! Just wait a little while until we can get things unpacked!"

A ripple of voices mixed with a chorus of mumbles rose from the crowd as Corbett fell silent.

Turning to Ki, Jessie said, "Well, he's trying to square things up, but I don't know whether or not the Indians will believe him, Ki. What do you think?"

"I think the Indians who could hear him might not believe him, and I'm sure that a lot who couldn't hear him wouldn't have believed him if they'd been able to hear," Ki replied.

"You say truth." The voice was that of a man behind them. He went on, "He has told so many lies before that they do not believe him now, when he tells them another one."

Jessie and Ki turned to look at the speaker. In spite of his almost scholarly tone of voice, his prominent high cheekbones and broad stubborn chin revealed his Sioux ancestry. Like so many of his race, he could have been any age from his middle twenties to a young forty, in that final period before maturity and experience had started to deepen and emphasize the lines on his face.

"Why do you say that?" Jessie frowned.

"My people have heard too many white man's lies before," the man replied. "They know the Indian Bureau is made up of thieves and liars who have nothing but hatred and contempt for our people."

"That's not all true," Jessie replied. "I know that there are liars and thieves in the Indian Bureau, just as there are almost everywhere, but there are honest men among them."

"If you say that, you do not know what has happened to our people, Miss Starbuck," the Indian replied. "Our people have been starved since the bureau took charge of our reservations and they are still starving. If you will give me the chance to prove this thing, Miss Starbuck, I will be glad to do so."

★

Chapter 10

A puzzled frown formed on Jessie's face, and for a moment all that she could do was to stare in amazement at the Indian. Then she found her voice and asked, "How did you know my name? I don't remember having seen you before, and I'm quite sure there's nothing wrong with my memory."

"And I also remember well," he said. His English was fluent, without the stumbling pauses and labored grammar which marked the speech of many tribesmen. "We have not met, Miss Starbuck, but I have seen you before. That was some years past, when you came with your father to the college in the East where I was a student."

Jessie's frown vanished and she nodded. "Of course!" she exclaimed. "The Carlisle Indian College! I remember going there on one of the last trips East that I made with my father. He was acting as an advisor to the college board. I'm surprised that you should remember me after such a long time. As I recall, there was quite a crowd that day."

"There were many people present, yes," the Indian went on. "And I can remember only a few of them. You are among the few. Perhaps it is because you have changed so little."

"I'm still astonished that your memory is so good," Jessie said. "I do remember going to Carlisle College with my father, but all that comes to mind now is being taken on a very extensive tour of the buildings and grounds while Alex was attending his meeting. I can't really recall much besides that."

"Perhaps it's easier for me to remember seeing you because there were so few of your people, and you were the only woman. To you, of course, I was just one of many young students."

"But if my father and I were there, Ki must have been too," Jessie said. Turning to Ki, she asked, "You were with Alex and me on that trip East, Ki, I haven't forgotten that."

"Yes, I went with you and Alex," Ki nodded. "But on the day when you went with him to Carlisle College, Alex had given me another job to do. It was quite urgent and had to be attended to at once, that's why I didn't go along."

"Then you couldn't've met—" Jessie stopped and turned to the Indian as she went on, "I started to introduce you to Ki without realizing that I don't even know your name."

"My Sioux name is Tesunke," the Indian said, extending his hand. Ki grasped it and as they exchanged handclasps the Indian went on, "It means Horse. But say my name in your language or mine, whichever you choose."

"My name's Ki," Ki put in quickly. "There's more to it, but most people find my full name a bit hard to handle."

"A name's only the shadow of a man," Tesunke nodded. "But it shortens the path to friendship."

"And it's convenient for all of us," Jessie said. "And while we're talking of names, if you don't mind, Tesunke, please don't call me anything except Jessie. For very good reasons, while I'm here on the reservation, I've shortened my last name temporarily to Star."

"I will not forget," he promised.

"Good," Jessie nodded. "And now that we've gotten all the formalities settled, I'd like to hear more about what you said a moment ago about the Indian Bureau starving your people. Can you prove it's true?"

"There should be no need to. You were watching when that bundle was opened a few minutes ago," Tesunke replied. "Is rotten meat and a handful of worms in a sack of flour what you would call food?"

"Certainly it isn't!" Jessie agreed. A frown formed on her face as she went on. "Is that the sort of ration all the tribes get from the Indian Bureau?" she asked.

"Most of the rations the Indian Bureau give us are bad," the Indian nodded. "I have not been here before, but I have been on others, and have heard those who know such things say that the food issued on this reservation is very bad indeed."

"Worse than it is on your reservations in Dakota Territory?" Jessie asked.

"From what I have seen here, I think it must be much worse," Tesunke said. "In Dakota Teritory, where I live, there are still a few buffalo herds. They are small now, not as big as they were when I was a boy, but each of our tribes is allowed to kill a few each year. One buffalo is not much for so many, but it is better than the beef we are issued."

"I'm sure these people here must have complained to the Indian Bureau about getting such bad rations," Jessie went on. "If I was—"

She stopped short as shouts burst out from the crowd that had now gathered in a wide cluster around Rafe Corbett and the Indians who were protesting the rations they'd received. Jessie could not hear Corbett's voice above the new commotion, but she could see the Indian Agency superintendent and the men nearest him, as the Indians moved and shifted around trying to get closer to him.

Corbett was shoving with hands and elbows as he attempted to keep from being engulfed, but the pressure of the shifting Indians around the edges of the crowd was almost irresistible. He was now almost hidden from sight, but he lowered one shoulder and started lunging from side to side, bending from the waist and using his shoulders as a battering ram as he tried to gain a bit of elbow room.

Suddenly a fresh outburst of shouts broke out from the Indians who were being pushed closer and closer to Corbett. One of the men, who until now had been in the vanguard of the protesters, turned and began shoving *away* from the Indian agent. The sudden reversal of their shoves took those furthest from the center of the growing fracas by surprise. Instead of giving ground they tried to push closer.

Jessie was the first to see the reason for the sudden commotion. Her eyes were fixed on Corbett, and as the Indians nearest him began drawing away she saw the Indian agent bring up his arm. Then she caught a glimpse of sunlight flashing from the blue steel barrel of the revolver in his hand. For a moment she thought of drawing her own Colt, but the crushing of the crowd caught her in its ripples as the Indians nearest Corbett started pushing away from him.

"Ki!" Jessie called. "Corbett's drawn his pistol! If he shoots one of these people it's sure to start a riot!"

Ki's response was instantaneous. He planted a hand on Tesunke's shoulder, and as he jumped and levered himself upward he somehow managed to take a *shuriken* out of his pocket. In the few seconds required for Ki to extract the blade, Corbett was bringing up his revolver.

While the Indian agent was still leveling his Colt, Ki's wickedly sharp throwing blade was flashing through the air. In spite of Ki's precarious position, his aim was as accurate as always. The star-pointed blade with its razor-edged cutting tips sliced into the bared wrist of Corbett's raised gun hand. Blood began oozing from the cut.

As the Indian agent's finger closed on the Colt's trigger, the pain in his wrist had already done the job Ki intended it to do. Corbett's instinctive flinching jerk raised the revolver's muzzle only a fraction of an inch, but that was enough to spoil his shot. The slug whistled harmlessly through the air. Its trajectory kept it high above the heads of the cluster of Indians around Corbett, and it went into the ground beyond the edges of the crowd without finding a human target.

Corbett's revolver shot had discouraged the Indians from crowding him. Even before its echoes had died away, those who'd been crowding up around the Indian agent were stepping back. They did not retreat, but moved far enough away to show that they had no more hostile intentions.

Instinctively, Corbett had brought up his left hand and clamped it over the gash cut on his wrist by Ki's *shuriken*. His revolver still dangled from his relaxed fingers, but now he could see that the danger of the Indians mauling him had passed. He'd begun making a clumsy effort to replace the weapon in its holster when Jessie, Ki, and Tesunke reached him.

"I'm sure that Ki will be glad to put your gun back in its holster while I get a handkerchief folded to bandage your wrist," Jessie said.

Wordlessly, Corbett allowed Ki to take the Colt that still dangled from his hand and restore it to its holster. Jessie was already pulling a bandanna from her pocket. She glanced at Ki and moved her head almost imperceptibly. Ki stepped back to join Tesunke, who'd stopped a pace or so away.

"Now hold out your hand so I can wrap this around it," Jessie went on. Her voice was neither friendly nor hostile.

Corbett stared at her, his jaw dropping, then he extended his hand as he said, "I got to say, Miss Star, you offering to fix this little cut I got, that's a real surprise. I figured you was on the Indians' side."

"I'm not on anybody's side," Jessie replied. She'd folded the handkerchief to form a thick, narrow strip, and as she began wrapping it around Corbett's hand she went on, "Our meetings haven't been what you could call cordial, but my only interest is—" she caught herself in time to remember her assumed identity, "the book I intend to write."

For a moment the Indian agent was silent, then he said, "I don't suppose you'll have much good to say about me, if you're figuring to put me into it at all."

"I haven't even started planning my book yet," she told him. "And until I find out all the hundreds of things I need to know, all I'll be doing is making notes."

"Well, I guess I owe you and that Chink you got tailing after you," Corbett said grudgingly. "I won't be standing in your way from now on. You go ahead and poke around all that you got a mind to. And if there's any questions you feel like you need to ask me, just feel free."

Though the Indian agent's changed manner had left Jessie almost speechless, she replied, "Thank you. There are some questions I'll need to ask you later, especially about the shocking state of the food you provide the Indians. That can wait, though. I'm sure that right now you'll want to see what can be done about giving these people the kind of rations they should be getting."

"If you're talking about the rotten meat laying over yonder, now that ain't really my fault. All I can give out is what I get shipped in, and I don't have any part of picking out what comes in the shipments."

"Then I'd strongly suggest you should inform your agency's headquarters of the problems you seem to be having and get the matter cleared up," Jessie said.

"It's a lot easier for you to say that than it is for me to do it. Like I said, all I can do is hand out what I'm sent," Corbett repeated as she finished tying the knot in the improvised bandage and stepped back. "I thank you for tying up that little scratch I got, Miss Star. I promise you that I'll keep in mind what we've been talking about."

"I'm sure you'll do what you can," Jessie nodded. She glanced around at the little cluster of Indians who still stood beside the pieces of spoiled meat and saw that Ki and Tesunke had edged up to stand at the edge of the group. She went on, "Now I have some matters to look after, so I'll leave you to solve your agency problems."

"You and the Indian agent seemed to be getting along pretty well, Jessie," Ki told her as she rejoined him and Tesunke. "I'm surprised, especially after that run-in we had with him up at the cabin."

"I'd rather have him on our side than working against us," Jessie said. "Besides, you know the old saying about honey catching more flies than vinegar."

"I would even be polite to him myself," Tesunke put in, "if I thought it would mean getting more food for our people."

"I don't believe it's entirely Corbett's fault for handing out bad food," Jessie said thoughtfully. "He's not the one who sends it here, and Washington is a long way from this isolated spot."

"Our people on the Dakota reservations are getting very angry," Tesunke went on. "And I am angry myself. This is one reason why I have come here."

"Suppose you explain some of the ways of your people so that I can understand them," Jessie suggested.

"I think that to understand our people's ways is hard for others," Tesunke said. "But I will try."

"Please do," Jessie said. Then she went on before Tesunke could answer, "I know just a little about your dances. There are some for hunting and others for fighting and—well, just about anything you do that is important."

Tesunke nodded. "Yes, dances and the chants that go with them are our lives. I am here to teach a new dance. It is to bring back the spirits of our old leaders, to help us now."

"And you've learned the dance from Wovoka?" Ki asked.

"Of course," Tesunke nodded. "He has been my teacher, and I have learned much from him. He is a great shaman." He hesitated for a moment, then added, "It is a powerful new medicine that Wovoka has brought us. This dance is one that was given to him when the sky ate the sun."

"You went to Carlisle, you're an educated man, Tesunke," Jessie said quickly when he paused. "You know the sky doesn't eat the sun. The moon just hides the sun now and then. You must understand about eclipses, I'm sure you must've learned why they happen when you were going to college."

"I have learned there what your people teach about the sun and the moon," he agreed. "But I was also taught other things that were not true."

"How can you say they're not true?" Jessie protested. "All the men who study things of that kind agree that the sun and the moon do go around the earth."

"There are things your people do not understand," Tesunke insisted. "Many of us have found out that our Old Ones, those you call medicine men, are wiser than the teachers who taught me things while I was at Carlisle." He hesitated for a moment, then went on, "You are a friend, Jessie, like your father was. I can trust you. I will tell you this much now. I have come here to teach others what Wovoka has taught me."

"About this Wovoka," said Ki. "Exactly what is it he's teaching?"

Now it was the Indian's turn to hesitate. He glanced at Jessie, who was frowning slightly, and then at Ki, who still stood expressionless. Neither of them tried to hurry his reply to Ki's question. At last Tesunke said,

"Wovoka is one of those given words of wisdom by the spirits of the first Sioux. They have taught him special prayers and dances that must be made to bring Wakan Tanka's spirit to our people—"

Jessie broke in. "I'm sorry to interrupt you, Tesunke, but when you went to college, surely you learned—"

Tesunke broke in quickly. "I learned much of the ways of your people. And I learned what happened when the soldiers from Mexico and the Black Robes first came here."

"But it's been a very long time since the Spanish came here," Jessie protested. "And even when they were here, they never did get far enough North to have trouble with the Sioux."

"That is true," he agreed. "But after the Black Robes were driven away, your people came to Sioux country with their guns and drove us out too. The Black Robes had taken our guns, and we could not fight them."

"It wasn't long before your people got guns to fight back with," Ki pointed out. "And things changed fast when you got good leaders like Crazy Horse and Sitting Bull."

"You have heard of them, then?" Tesunke asked.

"We've both seen their names in the newspapers we get from the East," Jessie explained. "They're still your chiefs, aren't they?"

"They are among the greatest of our leaders," he agreed. "Or they have been. Now Crazy Horse is dead and Sitting Bull has been made a prisoner."

"Yes," Jessie nodded. "Ki and I aren't completely unaware of what's been happening on the reservations, Tesunke."

"Then you know that Sitting Bull has been taken from his people by our soldiers?" Tesunke asked her.

136

"I haven't read anything about that in the papers, but I have heard about it," Jessie said. "And you're sure that Sitting Bull is still in jail?"

"He may not be locked behind bars," Tesunke answered. "But he is not a free man. It's possible that the soldiers are now taking him to a place where he will be held until your army decides there will be no trouble."

"Even with Sitting Bull a prisoner, there is some sort of trouble on the Sioux reservation, I've heard," Jessie said. "But I have two newspapers delivered to our ranch in Texas, and they always carry news of anything important that's happened, even on Indian reservations. There hasn't been a word in them about Sitting Bull."

"We've been away from the Circle Star quite a while, Jessie," Ki pointed out. "And we haven't seen a newspaper since we left Fort Worth."

"That's true, of course," she agreed. Turning back to Tesunke, she asked, "Tell me again: Why was Sitting Bull arrested?"

"There was trouble," Tesunke replied. "A quarrel with your generals about Wovoka's new dance. It is not a war dance. It is a dance that calls on the spirits—which you more than likely call ghosts. The Spirit Dance is to help our people live as we must do now."

"That certainly doesn't sound very dangerous to me," Jessie said. "Does it sound that way to you, Ki?"

Ki shook his head. "Not especially."

"And I do not think the dance is a bad thing," Tesunke said. "But there is a second dance I must also teach now, and it is not a war dance. It is the Spirit Dance, calling on the spirits of our great leaders to help our people."

"Do you plan to teach it here?"

"Of course," Tesunke replied. "Our people know the war dances, they must know this new one now.

"With Sitting Bull a prisoner, we have no great war chief to take his place. But we will win without Sitting Bull, for now we have Wovoka, and he has given us the Spirit Dance."

"But what kind of leader is he?" Ki put in. "You said he was a Paiute, so he couldn't be a Sioux war chief."

Tesunke stood silent again for several moments before replying. "It is foolish to call Wovoka a war chief. He is a great medicine chief. He has brought back to us the old spirits we had almost forgotten. To thank him for bringing them back, they made Wovoka a gift of a new dance and a new song."

"I hope that what you're telling us about aren't war songs and war dances," Jessie frowned. "I'm sure you learned when you were in school at Carlisle that your people and ours have to find a way to live together peacefully."

"Don't worry," Tesunke replied. "I have told you already that Wovoka is not a war chief. His dance is one that calls back the spirits of the Old Ones, the wise men who guided our people many years ago."

"I'm afraid I haven't visited often enough in the part of the country where the Sioux live to have learned about such things," Jessie frowned. "What do you call the 'Old Ones?' "

"They are the spirits who first taught our people to live in peace with your people," Tesunke said.

"What is the dance called?" Ki asked.

"We have named it the Sun Dance, for it is from a time when the sun smiled on all our people. And there is now a new dance to go with it. We call it the Spirit Dance, but your people have started to call it the Ghost Dance."

"And that's all?" Jessie frowned.

"That is all, Miss—Jessie," Tesunke replied.

"What I can't understand is why Sitting Bull was arrested," she went on. "Ki and I have traveled in much of Dakota Territory, I have a mine and some other business interests along the upper Missouri River, and I can't recall any trouble with the Indians on the reservations there."

"I am glad you say that," Tesunke told her. "This trouble is not with our people, but with our gods, our religion. I believe in them because I was taught to do so, and I have nothing else to believe in. I learned this long before I even dreamed I might attend Carlisle."

"Perhaps you'd better tell me a bit more about these new dances," Jessie suggested.

"I can only tell you what I learned," Tesunke replied. "But you would understand better if you saw and heard the dances."

"That would be impossible," Jessie replied. "I can't go all the way to Dakota Territory to watch a dance."

"I did not have that in mind," Tesunke said. "I've come here to teach the dances to our people on this reservation, and they are not secret, as so many in the army believe. If you are interested in learning, I am teaching a class tonight. Would you and Ki care to watch?"

★

Chapter 11

Jessie did not reply at once, the unexpected suggestion made so casually had taken her completely off-guard.

"You're sure that Ki and I would be welcome?" she asked at last. "I wouldn't want to be in your way during your lesson."

"You would not disturb the dancers," Tesunke assured her. "We have talked enough here for me to see that."

"Then I'll take your invitation, even if it does include a war dance," Jessie agreed. "Where will you go to teach your students?"

Tesunke pointed toward the river, indicating a thick stand of cottonwood trees as he said, "I have told my dancers to meet there after sunset. We will go to a place just beyond the trees where the dancers will not be seen from the agency and where there is room for them."

"Then Ki and I will be there," Jessie promised. "I

think it will be very interesting to watch your dance lesson."

"That is good," Tesunke nodded. "Now, I must go and tell some of the dancers to bring their war dance medicine bags as well as their Spirit Dance medicine. I have showed you where we will meet, I can do no more than that."

Tesunke started away. Jessie and Ki watched him for a moment or two, then Ki turned to her with a questioning look on his usually bland face.

"Why are you worrying, Ki?" she asked. "It's easy to see that something's bothering you."

"I'm just wondering if we should be at that dance lesson tonight, Jessie. Suppose the agency people hear the drums and chants and send men to stop it? We could get caught in the middle of an unpleasant fracas."

"I'm pretty sure the Indians who're camped here have sings and probably some medicine dances too," Jessie replied. "All we'll be doing is watch a few Indians learning a dance. It wouldn't be the first time. You remember the Hopi dance we were invited to watch when we visited their pueblo a few years ago."

"I also remember the Apache war dance we stumbled onto and the trouble we had because they thought we were spying on them," Ki reminded her.

"I certainly do remember that! If you hadn't been close enough to get me out of their hands, they might've had my scalp to add to their collection. But this isn't quite the same situation—we've been invited."

"Well, I'm as curious as you are, Jessie," Ki admitted. "And the chances are pretty good that tonight we'll learn more about the Indians and the way they get along with the agency than we would just by asking questions of those we'd run across in these little temporary camps they've made here."

"Of course we will," Jessie agreed. "But right now we'd better be thinking about food instead of dances."

"We've got enough of our saddle rations left for supper," Ki said. "And plenty of time. We can stop and eat whenever you want to."

"Even if I'm hungry, there's something I'd like to do before we think about supper. I'd like to have a little talk with Rafe Corbett," Jessie said. "We got off on the wrong foot with him in the beginning, and I'm wondering how he feels toward us after that nick you gave him with your *shuriken.*"

"It was just a scratch, and he didn't seem as gruff as usual when you were bandaging it, Jessie," Ki reminded her. "But I can understand why you'd want to talk to him before we go to the dance."

"Fence-mending has its place, Ki," she smiled. "And I have a hunch the time has come when Corbett will be very glad to be helpful, instead of acting like we're born enemies."

"Which will make quite a bit of difference in your report to Washington?"

"Of course," Jessie agreed. "I expected him to start blustering and threatening both of us when you nicked his hand. But it might've been that he decided it wasn't a good place or time to flare out at us with all those Indians standing around watching."

"It's possible," Ki nodded. He was looking ahead at the massive bulk of the Indian Agency building. "You know, Jessie, I hate to tell you this, but unless I'm mistaken we're not going to find Corbett or anybody else at the agency. From here the building looks deserted."

Jessie joined Ki in staring at the agency building,

and after a moment she said, "That's odd. I suppose it's possible they've closed early, but they couldn't have finished distributing the food in such a short time. There were still a lot of Indians waiting when we left."

"They'll be on the job again tomorrow, I'm sure. But I can't see how things will have changed much, unless there's a big stock of rations left to hand out."

"Let's start back toward the place where they'll be dancing, then," Jessie suggested. "On the way we're sure to find a good place to stop to rest while we eat a bite of supper. By then it'll be time to go on to that cottonwood grove and watch the dancers."

Dusk was already shadowing the eastern sky when Jessie and Ki drew near the the thick growth of tall cottonwoods. As they rode still closer they could hear an occasional drum-thump sounding beyond the grove. They tried to peer through the new growth of seedlings that rose head-high between and around the mature trees, but in the failing light they could see nothing beyond the screen of green leaves.

While the distance was shortening between them and the cottonwood grove, daylight continued to give way to darkness. They rode along the edge of the stand of trees until an occasional glint of firelight flickering beyond the foliage told them that they were close to their destination.

"We'd better tether our horses somewhere along the edge of this stand of cottonwoods, Ki," Jessie said. "If this dance is like most of those I've seen, there's going to be a lot of noise with it, drum-thumps, maybe some loud yelling."

"I suppose this is as good a place as any," Ki replied.

He pointed to a spot just ahead where the top of one giant cottonwood rose above the grove's smaller trees. "That's as good a place as any, I suppose."

Jessie nodded. "Yes. If these dances are drawn out as long a time as most of the Indian ceremonials, we may want to slip quietly away before it's finished."

By the time they'd reached the edge of the grove and tethered their horses, the occasional beating of the drum guided them. Skirting the thick belt of smaller trees around the bases of the tall cottonwoods, they rounded the grove. Now they could see the black silhouettes of figures moving against the firelight, and only a thin rim of bright sky remained in the west.

Even from a distance they could pick out the tall silhouette of Tesunke. He was moving through the group, stopping to exchange a few words or to take the hands and arms of one of the dancers and place them in a fixed attitude, or to move another dancer's feet and legs. It was obvious that he was showing them some posture or sequence of movements required by the dance they were learning.

"Tesunke has a lot more dancers than I'd expected to see," Jessie commented as they looked at the men who'd gathered around the small fire that had been kindled some distance from the margin of the cottonwood grove.

"There must be at least twenty of them," Ki said. "And from what we can see right now, most of them are young."

"So they are," she agreed. "Which probably means that he's chosen them because they'll live long enough to pass on the dance to the ones younger than they are right now."

Before Ki could reply, Tesunke saw them and waved.

He turned back to the youth he'd been instructing long enough to say a few more words, then started toward Jessie and Ki.

"You are just in time," he said as he came within easy speaking distance. "We are ready to start the dance. If you wish to see it best, you should go there," he pointed to a small ridge behind the fire, "and sit where the smoke will not drift to your faces."

"Anywhere you suggest, Tesunke," Jessie told him. She gestured toward the dancers, who were now gathering on the strip of level ground between the fire and the cottonwood grove. "I can see they're about ready to begin."

"Yes," he nodded. "I must go to them now. After the lesson, we will talk more."

Jessie and Ki walked the short distance to the tree Tesunke had indicated and made themselves comfortable on the high, soft grass. They watched as Tesunke stopped beside one of the Indians who'd stepped away from the others. The man was carrying a small drum, and he extended it to Tesunke, holding it while Tesunke tapped out a few beats. Then the drummer repeated the beats until Tesunke was satisfied with their rhythm and gestured for him to stop.

Waving to the dancers now, Tesunke waited while they gathered into a compact group, then motioned for the drummer to begin slapping his fingertips on the drum. He broke the rhythm once, corrected his error, and when he began tapping once more the dancers started moving in a slow circle to the drum's sharp beat. They moved slowly, and after a moment broke the silence with a throaty chant.

"I don't understand a bit of this, but I'm sure there's a meaning to every move they make," Jessie told Ki.

"Oh, of course," Ki replied. "And I wish that—"

He stopped when a loud shout sounded above the drumbeats. Beyond the dancers an Indian wearing only a breechcloth burst from the growth of trees and staggered into the bright circle of firelight. He was obviously exhausted. His steps were uneven and his chest was heaving. He waved toward the dancers. The drummer stopped beating and let his drum sag. The new arrival shouted a few words, then dropped to his knees. He lurched forward, falling into a crouch, his head dangling.

Tesunke had started for the unexpected newcomer the moment he'd appeared. The dancers broke their formation and followed Tesunke. Jessie and Ki had not moved during the moments after the new arrival's appearance. Now Jessie turned to Ki.

"That man's traveled a long way, Ki," she said. "Wherever he came from, something's happened to rouse the Indians. I'm very curious, of course, but I think it'd be wise for us just to sit here until Tesunke comes to tell us what this is all about."

"Yes, of course," Ki agreed. "That man's exhausted. It's pretty obvious that he's traveled a long way, so whatever his reason is for coming here must be very important to the Indians."

"A messenger," Jessie nodded. "I wonder if that man—or whatever message he's brought—might have anything to do with the Indian Agency office being closed? If something's happened that was really important, they'd have gotten word of it on their telegraph line."

"It's possible," Ki replied. Then he gestured toward the small group of Indians huddled around the unexpected arrival. "We'll learn very soon, Jessie. Tesunke's coming this way. I'm sure he's going to tell us what it's all about."

Tesunke was walking slowly toward them. The dancers who'd rushed to join him when the unexpected arrival had appeared were now helping the man, supporting him as they walked slowly toward the fire. Tesunke reached Jessie and Ki. He stopped, his face somber.

"That man has brought very bad news from the Sioux reservation in Dakota Territory," he said. He spoke slowly, as though each word carried a long-held grudge. "Hunkesheene, the great Sioux chief you call Sitting Bull, is dead. He was killed by the soldiers of his own people."

"His own people?" Jessie repeated. Shaking her head, she went on, "Surely nobody of the Sioux could have murdered their own chief!"

"Of this, I do not know," Tesunke said. "The man who brought the news here is very tired from his long hard trip. He has been carrying the word to other tribes—the talking drums of all the Sioux have been taken by the soldiers. The messenger has not yet told us anything more about what happened. When he rests and has food, he will tell us everything."

"Would you object if Ki and I stay here and listen to what he says?" Jessie asked. She hesitated for a moment, then added, "I'm not just asking out of idle curiosity, Tesunke. I have friends among the Sioux, as you know."

Tesunke frowned thoughtfully for a moment, then he said, "There is no reason why you should not stay. When the man has eaten and rested for a short while, he will tell us of how that bad day went. I do not think there was fighting on the Sioux reservation—he would have told us that much at once."

"We'll wait, then," Jessie nodded. "Just wave to us when the messenger is ready to tell his story."

Tesunke nodded and left to rejoin the other Indians. They had now helped the messenger to the fire and were standing around him. A few had produced food from their belt pouches and were offering it to the new arrival. After watching the group at the fire for a moment Jessie turned back to Ki.

"My guess when we saw the agency building closed was closer than I realized until now," she said. "The Indian Bureau must have sent telegrams to the Indian agencies telling them to close until the stir that's almost sure to follow Sitting Bull's death settles down."

"It's very likely," Ki agreed. "And we can be pretty sure there's going to be more than just a stir. Sitting Bull was one of the great Sioux war chiefs."

"My instructions from General Nesbitt certainly didn't cover a situation such as we're likely to be facing," Jessie said. "And I'm sure that in Washington right now the War Department is working with the Indian Bureau to keep things from exploding on the reservations."

"They've had plenty of time to work out some sort of plan," Ki said thoughtfully. "And that messenger must've been traveling for two or three days, perhaps longer."

"It's a long way," Jessie agreed. "Especially if he's stopped at other Indian reservations on the way here."

"There's been very little news about Indian activities in the papers we get at the Circle Star, Jessie. Have you noticed anything?"

Jessie shook her head. "The last time I read a newspaper story that mentioned Sitting Bull was just a short paragraph about the Indian unrest in Dakota Territory."

"I saw that too," Ki nodded. "And I wondered how much it didn't say. There was just a mention that Sitting Bull had been moved to Fort Yates—that's about in the middle of Dakota Territory."

"That unrest is what brought General Nesbitt to the Circle Star," Jessie said. "So what we're up against now is trying to figure out what we need to do. But let's listen to what the man who just came here has to say. If we're lucky, we'll get some sort of clue that we can use as a guide."

"We're not going to have a long wait," Ki told her. He pointed toward the fire where the silhouetted figures of the dancers were beginning to gather into a circle.

"We won't wait for Tesunke to invite us to join them, then," Jessie said. "Let's just go up and stand quietly, be as unobstrusive as possible."

Sunset had passed by now and darkness was setting in. Jessie and Ki made their way to the fire. The dancers had taken off their headdresses and were hunkered down in a wide arc. By the fire, facing the waiting group, Tesunke stood by the messenger. The newcomer was a tall, wiry man, with a thin, hawk-nosed face. His narrow lips were pressed soberly together.

He was dividing his attention between the dancers and Tesunke, and when he saw Jessie and Ki approaching he turned to Tesunke and said something, his voice so low that Jessie and Ki could hear only a murmur. Tesunke's reply was in the Sioux tongue, and neither Jessie nor Ki could make out any of it. At last the messenger shrugged and turned to face the dancers.

"Bad news I bring," he began. "But all our people must hear truth of what has taken place."

A stirring murmur of voices rose from the dancers and Tesunke gestured for them to be silent. Using the shield of the momentary noise, Jessie whispered to Ki, "That messenger didn't like us being here, but Tesunke seems to've persuaded him to let us stay and hear what he has to say."

Before Jessie had finished, the messenger started to talk again and Ki only nodded in response to Jessie's observation.

"Our great chief *Hunkesheene* did not die in a fight against our enemies, the ones he fought so many times before," the messenger went on. "In the time before he was killed he had stayed in his cabin many days. He did not go to the camps of our people, though there were many tepees all around him, and our fighting men were waiting for him to send for them, so they could come together and go to meet our enemies and kill them."

Again the voices of the listening dancers broke out in subdued exchanges, and again Tesunke gestured for them to be quiet. The murmurs faded slowly to a low undercurrent of hushed voices, but the messenger seemed not to notice them. He raised his voice and resumed his narration.

"There were fighters from the whites around the cabin of our great Hunkesheene, but for many days they did nothing. Then word came that he must go to another place, where he would be put in prison. The whites did not go to Hunkesheene's cabin. They sent the chiefs of our own Sioux police to get him. The police went and told Hunkesheene he must come with them. He told them he would go, and ordered his own warriors to saddle his finest horse. Then he went out of his cabin with the men who had come to tell him, and when he saw so many soldiers waiting, he stopped outside the door and stood still."

After his long speech the messenger stopped to breathe. No sound—not a voice—was raised. The crowd of listeners did not move.

"When Hunkesheene did not move forward," the messenger continued, "the police were not happy. Some of them moved, and raised their guns, then someone called out, 'Shoot the police who guard Hunkesheene, the others will run in fear!' No one knows who said this thing, it may have been Hunkesheene himself who spoke. But then one of the Sioux who was with the watchers shot, and the police who were guarding Hunkesheene raised their rifles and shot, and Hunkesheene fell. When the Sioux who were watching saw him fall, they began shooting and the two men of the police fell beside him, and they were dead too."

Once again the narrator stopped to breathe. Not a sound came from the listening dancers. When the messenger spoke again his voice was harsh.

"This is a true thing I tell you! I saw it happen just as I have told it to you!"

His words triggered the watchers. Some of them had moved closer to the fire while the messenger was telling his story, and now most of the men nearest the narrator were getting on their feet, moving toward him. The noise of their voices grew louder by the moment and Jessie turned to Ki.

"I think this is the time when we'd better leave," she said. "The more these Indians hear of Sitting Bull's death, the angrier they're going to get."

"Yes, and the news is going to spread fast," Ki replied.

He gestured toward the circle of light cast by the waning fire. Jessie turned to look and saw that while several of the dancers were moving toward the messenger, others were heading for the area where the Indian camps were thickest. Then she turned back to Ki.

"It might be wise for us to retreat all the way to our cabin," she suggested. "Our horses haven't been worked too hard, and we haven't any idea how long the Indian Agency's going to be closed. We'll give things a chance to settle down here, and plan to come back late tomorrow or early the next day."

★

Chapter 12

"You know, Ki, there's something that makes a person feel comfortable when they have four walls and a roof between them and the outdoors," Jessie said.

She looked around the raw boards that glowed softly, the pine wood shining reddish gold in the light of the candle on the floor between them.

"Especially when there's no way to predict what might happen tomorrow," Ki agreed. "Your idea to build it came just at the right time."

"Perhaps it did," Jessie agreed. Then she shook her head and went on, "But my idea came to me before we had any notion of this Indian trouble. Our little cabin's a long way from being a fort, Ki."

"Even so, we shouldn't have too much to worry about here," Ki replied. His voice was thoughtful as he added, "For one thing, the Indians don't know we're here. For another, their quarrel's with the Indian Agency men, not with us."

"That's true enough, but fighting's a fever, Ki,"

Jessie said somberly. "And with the agency office deserted, the Indians just might decide we're enemies and attack us."

Ki nodded, then he said, "It's easy to understand why we found the agency office closed. Rafe Corbett and his crew weren't taking any chances. Thinking back, they must've gotten word to leave before the Indians heard anything about Sitting Bull being killed."

"That's quite possible," Jessie nodded. "You remember that General Nesbitt told us about a special underground telegraph line for emergency use. Some army officer up in Dakota Territory must've notified Washington on the military telegraph about Sitting Bull being killed, and then the Indian Bureau sent a telegraph message notifying Fort Supply."

"Telling them to close the agency office? To go find a safe place to hide until it was safe to open it again?"

"Quite possibly both," Jessie nodded. "Remember how easy it is to start a panic in Washington. The only reason we're here now is because somebody in the army got nervous about the Indian Bureau—or maybe it was the other way around—and sent General Nesbitt to the Circle Star—"

"And the general came and enlisted you to look around the reservations because someone was nervous about them," Ki concluded for her. He was smiling as he went on, "But in this case the nervousness was justified. I know how it is. There've been a lot of times when I've heard your father say just about what you're saying now."

"I couldn't very well refuse the general, Ki," Jessie went on. "And there wasn't any way for us to look into the future, or to predict what might happen."

"Of course not. And now that it's happened, we can do one of two things."

"I'm sure I know what you're suggesting, Ki," Jessie nodded. "We can go on, or we can go back to the Circle Star. But I'm not inclined to be in a hurry to do either one tonight. Let's sleep on it, and see how things look tomorrow."

"We should be able to find out more tomorrow," he agreed. "As soon as the Indians learn what really happened—that Sitting Bull was shot by accident—they'll probably settle down."

"Do you think that's going to matter, if the Indians get aroused enough and angry enough?"

"I think that's something only time can answer," Ki replied. "But we should know tomorrow. It's going to take quite a while for the truth about Sitting Bull's death to spread."

"I'm sure you're right about that," she agreed. "But by tomorrow things should've quieted down. Let's get some sleep, now. We'll see what it looks like at the agency the first thing in the morning."

"Just to be safe, I'm going to put the horses where they can't be seen from the road," Ki told her.

"That will only take you a minute or two," Jessie said. "I'll leave the candle for you to blow out. I'm suddenly so sleepy that I don't think it'll bother me."

"Whatever you choose," Ki replied. "But I'll have my night vision by the time I get the horses around on the other side of the cabin."

Ki stood for a moment and let his eyes adjust to the starlight glow. Then he untethered the horses and led them around the little shanty to the small, bare area behind it, where they could not be seen from the road.

He started back to the cabin door and had almost reached it when thudding hoofbeats sounded in the distance. Taking a *shuriken* out of the pocket at his vest, Ki stepped into the deep shadows that shrouded the end of the cabin. The hoofbeats grew louder, and he leaned away from the shadows, trying to catch sight of the rider who was approaching. The distance between the road and the cabin was not great, but trying to make out details in the darkness was impossible even for Ki's sharp eyes.

Suddenly the rhythm of the hoofbeats changed. They slowed, then stopped on the stretch of road just below the cabin. Ki was taking full advantage of his cover now. He held his *shuriken* ready and leaned forward just enough to enable him to see the darkness-distorted forms of the horse and its dismounting rider. Then the man who'd swung out of the saddle called, and he recognized the voice of Rafe Corbett.

"Hello, the cabin!" Corbett shouted. "Don't get all nerved up and start shooting! It's me, Rafe Corbett, Miss Star! There's something important I need to talk to you about!"

Ki was baffled only for a fraction of a second, until he remembered that Jessie had shortened her name for this mission. Before he could move or speak, Jessie was replying.

"Come on up to the cabin, then," she said. "I can't imagine what you have to say, but I'll listen to you."

Ki reached the cabin door a moment before Corbett did. Jessie was standing just inside. Corbett saw them in the dim glow of light from the single candle that burned in the cabin. Ki gestured for the Indian agent to step in first.

"I hope I ain't bothering you, busting in this way

at night and all," Corbett said as he entered the little shelter. His voice had lost its old bluster—it was that of a worried man.

"Not at all," Jessie said cooly. "But I'm quite curious to find out your reason for coming here. Do you need help taking care of some of your men at the agency? The Indians were in a fighting mood last night, I do know that much."

"No, it ain't that," Corbett replied. "We got a hidey-hole that opens off the cellar. Nobody much but us knows about it, and me and the crew followed our standing orders to hole up if trouble starts. That's what we did. I'm the only one that's come out, the rest of the men's still in there."

"You must've come here for a reason," Jessie said.

"Oh, sure," the agent replied. "I wasn't real certain I'd be welcome, and I still don't know for sure if I'm doing the right thing. You come down to it, the fact of the matter is, I'm sorta between a rock and a hard place."

"Suppose you explain, then," Jessie suggested.

"Well, for one thing, I'm breaking my standing orders. I'm not supposed to leave the agency building while there's trouble like this, but you're the only one I could think of that might lend me a hand."

"A hand doing what?"

"Why, I noticed the other day that you and your hired man there was pretty good riders. I punched cattle and herded a couple of drives from a ranch to a stockyard, and the way you set a horse gave me the idea you and him might know something about handling cattle."

"Both Ki and I have had experience on a ranch," Jessie nodded. "But what's that got to do with the trouble you're having?"

"Miss Star, there's just one thing that's going to settle things down at the agency," Corbett said. "And that's fresh meat to hand out to the redskins."

"I'm sure you're right about that," Jessie said. "But what has that to do with me?"

"After I'd thought a lot about what to do, I've come to you because I figure you're about the only ones around here I can trust. I'm breaking orders just getting away from the agency building, but what I've got in mind can't wait."

Corbett paused. From the worried frown on his face it was apparent that he was searching for words. Jessie prompted him.

"Go on, Mr. Corbett," she said. "I'll listen to whatever it is you have to say."

"Well," Corbett began, "Me and my clerks are all going to be holed up a while. We'll give the redskins a couple of days to settle down, then we'll start trying to smooth things down. It won't be easy, but that's where you're the only one I could think about to ask for a little help."

"What kind of help?" Jessie asked. "Is someone hurt?"

"Not yet, and I hope nobody will be, Miss Star," the Indian agent replied. "But maybe I better start from the first and tell you why I'm here."

"That would be a very good idea," Jessie nodded. Her voice was cool, but not overtly unfriendly. "When I'm asked for help without first being told what kind of help is needed and why, I'm inclined to refuse."

"Maybe what I got to say won't change your mind about the way our outfit's been cheating the redskins, but all I been doing is what my boss in St. Louis has put me on standing orders to do," Corbett began. "I reckon it's the same as all the other agency stations does. You see, when we get a shipment of spoiled rations, we go right ahead and hand it out just like it was good."

Though she'd been warned by General Nesbitt about graft in the agency, Jessie had been inclined to place the blame on greedy or crooked agents. Now that Corbett was about to give her a word-picture of a chain of cheating and embezzlement, Jessie was getting a glimpse of the full picture. She felt that her eyes were being opened for the first time.

"Those were your orders from the agency's office in Washington?" she asked.

"We're supposed to hand out the rations regardless of whatever shape they're in," he replied. "Good, bad, or middling, rotten meat or fresh. We ain't allowed to complain to nobody, and we ain't supposed to tell nobody about what I just told you."

"Are you positive that other agents have the same orders you got?" Ki asked.

"I wouldn't have a way to prove it, but I'd make a pretty close guess that's how it is," Corbett replied.

"If you're not in a position to expose something of that sort, I am," Jessie told him as her mission and the false identity she'd assumed popped into her mind. "It would make good material for my book."

"Sure, I tumbled to that from the first time you told me what you're doing here," Corbett nodded. "But that can wait till later. Right now, I've got too much else to think about."

"Suppose you tell us what it is, then," she suggested.

"There's only one way I can see to quiet down that ruckus at the agency, Miss Star," Corbett went on. "And that's to give the Indians a good ration of fresh meat."

"Just where are you planning to get fresh meat?" Jessie asked. "Can you order it over your telegraph line? And how long will it be until it gets here?"

"That's where you and your man come in, don't you see?" the Indian agent replied. "I've brought along every penny of cash that was in the agency safe, and I figured you and him could take it to the closest ranch and buy two, maybe three steers with it, to give to the Indians."

"I'll have to admit that I'm surprised to find you so thoughtful," Jessie said. Then she asked, "I suppose you know where the closest ranch is? And I suppose you know what kind of a job's involved in driving just a few steers, not enough to make up a real herd?"

"I got to admit I don't know where a ranch is," Corbett replied. "And there's not a man in my bunch that knows how to drive steers in either. I know that, because I asked 'em before I started out to come here."

"Ki and I don't know any more than you do about the location of a ranch in this vicinity," Jessie said. "But I imagine there must be one or two fairly close by."

Ki had been silent during the conversation between Jessie and Corbett. Now he said, "We can find out very easily if there's a cattle ranch anywhere near, Jessie."

"How?" she asked.

"Why, the storekeeper up the road will know," he replied. "Or the girls in the bawdyhouse that's on the road to the store, they'd be able to tell us."

"Of course they would," Jessie agreed. "And they wouldn't be in a place that's so far away from anywhere unless they had enough visitors to make it profitable, or unless they depend on the men from the agency to keep them busy."

162

"They don't get any customers from my crew, Miss Star," Corbett assured her. "My men know that if they set foot off the agency grounds they'll be fired."

After another moment or two of thought, Jessie nodded and said, "All right, Mr. Corbett. I know you have enough trouble on your hands, and I'm sure that if you can offer the Indians some fresh beef that trouble will stop as quickly as it started. Ki and I will help you all we can."

"I'm sure glad to hear you say that, Miss Star," Corbett replied, heaving a big sigh of relief. He reached into his pocket and took out a leather poke. As he handed it to Jessie he went on, "I don't know to a penny how much money's in this, because I didn't take time to count it, but I'd guess there's enough to buy a few steers."

"I'll count it and give you a receipt for what we've spent," Jessie said as she took the poke. "And I'll drive the best bargain that I—" She broke off as yells sounded outside the cabin.

"Indians," Ki said quickly. "Something that we don't know about must've happened on the reservation."

"Damned if I know what it could be," Corbett said. "Unless they've broken into the building and found my crew. They'd know where I am, and the redskins've got ways to make my clerks talk."

Outside, the first few shouts had now been reinforced by a chorus of quivering high-pitched cries. A rifle barked, and its slug lodged itself into a tree trunk on the steep slope just below the cabin.

Jessie said quickly, "The light, Ki! Blow it—"

She stopped short when she saw that Ki was already reaching for the candle. The yells from the road were increasing in volume now as Ki pulled the candle out of the little clot of wax drippings that held it in place. He was extinguishing it when another shot rang out from the trail. The rifle's bullet splintered the roof boards, whistled across the cabin, and buried itself in the opposite wall.

Ki did not have time to blow out the candle before the next shot cracked above the increasingly loud shouts from the direction of the road. Corbett lurched forward, a gasp of pain breaking from his lips as he crumpled to the floor. Both Jessie and Ki started toward him, but when another rifleshot sounded from the road and the bullet splintered the wall just above the level of their heads, they dived to flatten themselves on the floor beside Corbett.

Ki was still trying to get a firm grip on the candle, but the slippery wax film on its surface defeated his best efforts. The little cylinder slid from his hands as he hit the floorboards. The candle rolled a few inches before its flame flickered and died, leaving the cabin in darkness.

Jessie had already begun rolling across the floor toward the corner where she'd placed her rifle as the cracks of two more shots, then a third, sounded outside. The yells outside were increasing in both volume and number now. Jessie groped along the wall in the darkness until her hands found the butt of her Winchester.

She twisted to sit erect as her eyes sought the sky-lighted door opening. Shouldering the rifle, she fired one shot, knowing as she triggered it off that it would be wasted, but hoping that a show of resistance from the cabin might dampen the enthusiasm of the Indians yelling from the sloping ground between the cabin and the road. If anything, the shouts grew louder, and the crack of two shots broke through above the angry yells on the slope below. Neither of the slugs hit the cabin, and Jessie began inching toward the door.

"Ki!" she called, raising her voice to be heard above the increasingly loud war cries from the road. "Where are you?"

"Just inside the door," he replied. "I'll be able to see the first men that come up the slope and I've got my *shuriken* ready!"

"I'll hold my fire, then," Jessie told him. "But get away from the door fast when the first Indians show up, because I'm waiting and ready!"

Ki did not reply, but Jessie needed no answer. She and Ki had faced perils much greater than the attacking Indians. They had learned to protect themselves and to work as a team during their long series of encounters with the merciless gunmen of the European cartel that had been trying to seize control of the Starbuck industrial empire created by her father. Jessie settled back, waiting for the first silhouettes to appear against the star-bright night sky.

During the minute or less Jessie and Ki had been talking, the din of shrill threatening yells had not diminished. The outcries rose in volume, and Jessie kept her eyes fixed on the doorway. Her vision had adjusted to the darkness now. She could see the silhouetted foliage of the two or three trees on the slope between the cabin and the road, but as yet no human form had appeared, and there had been no shots fired from the attacking Indians.

Suddenly the silence was shattered by a gunshot, then another. Bullets splintered the wall of the cabin, but tore through the roof instead of the wall below it. The brief volley was not repeated, but the threatening cries of the attackers still broke the night's stillness.

Suddenly and unexpectedly the yells diminished, then stopped. The voice of a single man reached Jessie's ears, but his words were in one of the Indian languages, one strange to her. A babble of voices, impossible to understand, broke the night when he stopped. The small din died away and the man who'd been doing the talking was also silent. Then he spoke again.

"Jessie!" he called.

Now Jessie could recognize his voice. It was Tesunke who called her, and she could not hold back the sigh of relief that escaped her lips.

"Jessie!" Tesunke repeated. "You don't have anything to worry about now!"

"I hear you, Tesunke," she called. "And I don't know when I've been as relieved to hear anybody call me as I am right now!"

"Strike a light," Tesunke said. "I'm coming up to talk to you. Don't worry about the men who've been giving you trouble, they're on their way back to the reservation."

★

Chapter 13

"You don't know how glad I am to see you, Tesunke!" Jessie exclaimed.

She was standing in the doorway, Ki just behind her, holding the unlighted candle in one hand and a match in the other, waiting for Tesunke to take the last few steps up the slope to the cabin. As he reached the door, she struck the match and touched it to the wick of the candle.

"I didn't realize how much trouble there'd be until the shooting started down on the reservation," Tesunke said. "Then I started looking for you and Ki, but until I'd covered all the area around the agency building and found out that Corbett had started up to your cabin I didn't realize you must've left earlier than I'd expected you to."

"There are a few things we didn't realize, either," Jessie replied. "Not until Corbett came up here."

She stepped back into the cabin to allow Tesunke

167

to enter. He looked past her and saw Corbett's body sprawled on the floor.

"He's dead!" Tesunke exclaimed. "I certainly didn't expect that my dance lesson would end this way!"

"It wasn't just your dance lesson that caused all of this," Jessie assured him. "Everything started with the rotten meat rations the agency men were trying to force on the Indians. The trouble was there all the time, just waiting for something to trigger it off."

"Corbett came up here to talk to Jessie," Ki said when she fell silent. "The Indians were following him. They were angry. I think the rotten meat that the agency had given them is really responsible for the trouble starting, and then growing bad as quickly as it did."

"You're very likely right, Ki," Tesunke agreed. "From what some of my dancers told me, I got the idea that this isn't the first time the ration meat's been bad."

Jessie said quickly, "No, it isn't. Corbett admitted that. He came up here to ask Ki and me to go to the nearest ranch and buy some steers. He gave us the money to pay for them, and wanted us to drive them here so he could make another ration distribution as soon as we got back."

"Is there a ranch close by, then?" Tesunke asked.

"We shouldn't have any trouble finding out," Ki put in. "Jessie had agreed that we would go. We were just getting ready to start out when the people from the reservation got here."

"And even if Corbett's dead, you intend to do what he asked you to?"

"Of course," Jessie replied. "When I give my word to do something, I'll honor my promise. That's one of the many things Alex taught me."

"Then if you're going, I'll go with you," Tesunke said. "I know enough about driving cattle to help."

"What about your lessons teaching the new dancers?" she asked. "Are you going to give them up?"

"No. But I think it might be well to delay a few days before I start them again," Tesunke answered. "The need for them isn't going to change, and, besides, the people here on the reservation aren't going to settle down for several days."

"Ki and I will certainly be glad to have you go with us," Jessie said. "We'd planned to start as soon as possible. Will you need to go back to the reservation for anything?"

Tesunke shook his head. "No. I carry all that I need in my saddle pouches, and I hadn't picked out a place to spread my blankets when the trouble started."

Ki turned to Jessie and asked, "After this busy day we've had, do you feel like starting tonight? Or should we rest and start fresh in the morning?"

"I don't feel at all tired or sleepy," Jessie replied. "Is there any reason for us to change our plans?"

"None that I can see," Ki replied. "And if one of us feels tired, we can always stop by the trail—if there even is a trail—and rest until daylight."

"Then let's go right on, as we'd planned to do," Jessie suggested. She turned to Tesunke and asked, "Is that all right with you? Or do you want to put off leaving until daylight?"

"I see no reason to delay," he said, shaking his head. "Unless there might be trouble following an unfamiliar trail in the dark."

"That shouldn't bother us too much," Jessie assured him. "We'll stop at the little ghost town up the road and talk to the storekeeper. I'm sure he'd know what the trail's like to the nearest ranch. If we're really in luck, he'll be able to give us all the information we need."

Jessie, Ki, and Tesunke had talked very little since riding away from the cabin. The quarter-moon, dropping now in its short arc to the horizon, brightened the night sky barely enough for them to follow the trail. While the land was level they'd ridden abreast, but on the broken upslope which their horses were now mounting the trail narrowed, and they rode single file with Jessie in the lead.

Topping the slope, Jessie glanced at the level land ahead and reined aside to let Tesunke and Ki pull up abreast of her. Tesunke gestured ahead, where a rectangle of reddish light showed on the front of the square house silhouetted against the sky.

"If that's the light of the grocery store ahead, it must really be an unusual establishment," he observed.

"You know quite well that isn't a store, Tesunke," Jessie said. "But we're only a little way from the town now. Another few minutes—" Jessie broke off and a new thoughtful note came into her voice as she continued, "Seeing that place gives me an idea, though. Most of its customers probably come from the Indian Agency, but if there's a ranch close by, the hands must patronize it too."

"And if we stop and ask, the women would quite likely be able to give us directions to the ranch," Ki said. "Then we wouldn't waste time trying to wake up the storekeeper when we get to his place."

Ki and Tesunke started speaking at the same time, both agreeing with her. When the confusion of their mingling voices ended, Jessie said, "The women in that bawdyhouse won't try to solicit me as a customer the way they would if either of you went in. It'll save time if I go and ask them if there's a ranch close by."

During their brief exchange they'd almost reached the house, and as they pulled up in front of it a few minutes later Jessie swung out of her saddle, walked to the door, and tapped on it. The door opened after a few moments to silhouette a woman against the strip of light that spilled from the room behind her.

"Ain't your friends coming in?" the woman asked, glancing first at Jessie, then at Ki and Tesunke in their saddles.

"They're not customers," Jessie told her. "We're looking for the nearest ranch, and thought you might be able to tell us if there is one close by, and how we can get to it."

"Now, wait a minute!" the woman exclaimed. "If you're figuring on setting up some pasture tricks, you got another think coming! We got a deal with all the ranchers inside of a day's ride from here—"

"Please!" Jessie broke in, "We're trying to find a ranch where we can buy a steer or two. I don't have time to do a lot of explaining, but we're in a hurry."

"Well, I sure don't know what this is all about, but if you're looking for a ranch, the closest one is the Crossed Ts. It's about six miles away from here."

"Which way do we go to find it?"

"Just follow your nose, honey. Take the first fork to the right you come to after you get through town and keep on going. It ain't a bad trail. You'll see the Crossed Ts' main house after you've rode maybe three or four hours." The woman paused for a moment, then asked, "You mind telling me what all this to-do's about? We heard an awful lot of yelling and goings on from down by the agency building. Has the redskins been cutting up, or something like that?"

"I'm afraid it would take too much time to explain," Jessie said. She was opening her belt pouch as she spoke. Fumbling the coins in it she found a double eagle and took it out. Handing it to the woman, she went on, "Thank you for your help. We're in a hurry, so we won't bother you any longer."

Rejoining her companions, Jessie told them, "We just might be in luck. There's a ranch within a three-or four-hour ride. At this time of the year they're likely to have good-sized herds waiting to go to market."

"That sounds encouraging," Ki said. "If we push on as fast as we can without tiring the horses, we ought to be able to start back late tomorrow morning."

"And with luck, we will be driving a few steers," Tesunke nodded. "Fresh meat will do more good than anything I can think of to calm down my people on the reservation."

"I only wish it was as easy to drive four steers as it is to drive a big cattle herd," Jessie remarked as she sat with Ki and Tesunke around their small supper fire.

They had stopped for the night in a narrow arroyo after a day which had begun at first dawnlight, the sun was just beginning to show its edge above the horizon when they started driving the four steers away from the main house of the ranch where they'd bought them. Jessie gestured toward the animals huddled in a small enclosure improvised from the lariats which she and Ki always carried.

Jessie went on, "These are the contrariest steers I've ever handled. Even if there are only four of them, they've given us a lot more trouble than some of the big herds I've seen."

"Trouble or not, it is a good thing that we have the animals," Tesunke said as he looked at the steers, pressed close together in the makeshift pen. "Good fresh meat, not rotten beef such as my people have been given, will do a great deal to wipe away their anger. What we are doing should go far toward bringing peace back to the agency."

"I'm certainly not complaining, Tesunke," Jessie told him quickly. "I know the people on the reservation have been treated very badly in the past. But I'm sure the Indian Bureau will do something at once to keep that from happening again."

"Yes, things should change in a lot of ways," Ki said. "I know that, and Jessie does, but we're not supposed to talk about it. You'll just have to take our word that there will be a number of changes." Ki was standing up as he talked. He went on, "Now, I'm going to walk and use my leg muscles. They've gotten stiff from being bent too long in the stirrups."

As Ki disappeared into the darkness, Tesunke turned to Jessie and said, "Perhaps we should do as Ki is, and walk around for a little while before we go to our blankets."

"A good idea," Jessie agreed. "My legs need to be used too. And the steers are secure, we won't need to worry about them wandering away."

They started out, strolling companionably in the last moments of the fast-ending day. They said nothing during the first few minutes of their slow, leisurely walk, but before the silence between them grew oppresive, Jessie turned to Tesunke and said, "There's been so much happening since we met that we've really had very little time to talk. Do you spend your time moving from one place to another? Or do you have a home and wife and perhaps children?"

"I have not taken a wife," Tesunke replied. "Not because it is forbidden for me to marry, but because I have still to find the woman I would wish to be with all the time."

"If you had said man instead of woman, you could've been describing the way I feel," Jessie smiled.

"It is not that women do not come into my life," he went on. "Our people do not follow the customs of yours, as you very likely know. We give no shame to a man who lays with a woman, and none for a woman who invites herself to go with a man to his blankets."

"Even if they have known one another for only a short time?"

"Not even if they have only seen one another more than a day or perhaps less."

"That's about as long as we've seen one another," Jessie smiled. "Unless you count that time when we met at Carlisle."

"Both of us had other things to think of then," Tesunke said. "And we were very young. Besides that, we were never alone together there during the time after we met."

"But this is different, isn't it?"

"Very different," he agreed. "And I have been traveling from one tribe to another, with too little time to think of sharing a blanket with a woman. I have had in my mind nothing but the message I have been carrying."

"Then you wouldn't say no, if I felt like inviting you to my blanket?" Jessie asked.

"That is the question I was about to ask you," Tesunke replied. "But what about Ki?"

"Ki and I aren't lovers. We've never been. He doesn't talk to me about women, and though he knows that I enjoy being with a man, he's never said a word to me about the times I've spent with any of them."

"It's well that we understand each other," Tesunke told her. "We have no blanket, but shall I spread my shirt?"

"Your shirt and my skirt spread on the ground together would make a very satisfactory bed," she agreed.

They'd been slowing the pace of their walk bit by bit as they were talking, and during their exchange of intimacies they'd come to a complete stop. Total darkness shrouded the prairie now, but their eyes had adjusted to the fading daylight. Jessie tugged the knot of her sash cord to free it, and Tesunke began unbuckling his pistol belt. He dropped the belt and holster to the ground and skinned his buckskin jacket over his head. They patted and tugged the skirt and jacket together to form a thin cushion on the low prairie grass.

Straightening up, Tesunke had begun tugging at the knot of the narrow strip of leather that served him as a belt when Jessie reached out to move his hand away. She freed the knot and begun to push the waistband of the supple deerskin garment down his hips. Tesunke did not try to help her, but stood motionless while she worked the trousers downward until his erection was freed and jutting.

Now Jessie moved her hands to the swollen cylinder, as round as her wrist and almost the length of her forearm. She began caressing it gently with her fingertips. Tesunke ended her soft stroking by sliding his hands up her sides to lock them under her armpits and lift her

175

off her feet. He held her in midair for only a moment, long enough for Jessie to bring up her legs and lock her ankles around his waist.

Holding her close to him with an arm encircling her, Tesunke dropped to his knees. He bent forward and Jessie released her embrace, allowing herself to slide down to the blanket. She wriggled for a moment to grow accustomed to her new posture, then relaxed her leg-grip.

Tesunke was now poised above her, bending forward. The moon was at his back, darkening his face and body. Jessie brought up her hand to pull his head down and bring their lips together, but Tesunke lifted his head when he felt the pressure of her hand.

"No, Jessie," he said softly. "It is not the way of my people to kiss at such a moment."

"Then do as your people do," she said, allowing her body to relax as much as possible. She spread her thighs wide and was slipping her hand between their bodies, reaching to place him when Tesunke grasped her wrist.

"No," he said. "That is for the man to do!"

While he spoke Tesunke was shifting a bit, kneeling between Jessie's outspread thighs. He slid his arm between them and after a moment of fumbling, placed himself.

Jessie was not expecting Tesunke's sudden thrust when he drove into her. His lunge and his full penetration brought a gasp of surprise bursting from her lips, and involuntarily she twisted her hips and tried to raise them. Tesunke was resting his full weight on her now, quick ripples of pleasure mixed with pain swept through her body. Then the pain ebbed, and only pleasure remained as Tesunke raised himself a bit and pounded with a second fierce lunge. Jessie loosed a gasp of pleasure as he drove into her until his stroke was completed.

"You're filling me completely, Tesunke!" she exclaimed. "Go gently now, until I can get used to—"

"Don't worry," Tesunke broke in. "I do not want to hurt you, only to give you as much pleasure as you give me."

Jessie did not reply. She was moving her hips slowly, rolling them from side to side as she tried to get accustomed to the sensation that was rippling through her supine form.

Now Tesunke began lunging, long, trip-hammer drives with no pauses between them. Thrust followed thrust at a tempo which Jessie had seldom experienced. For a moment she tried vainly to match her timing with his, but could not raise her hips quickly enough to bring them up with the speed of Tesunke's fierce, fast drives. She loosened the grip that until this time she'd managed to maintain, and sprawled her thighs as widely as she could while Tesunke continued his fierce drives.

Much more quickly than she'd ever dreamed possible, Jessie was shuddering into a spastic climax. Tesunke paid no attention to her writhing twists and her throaty cries of the almost unbearable pleasure that was seizing her. He continued his fast, fierce thrusting, and Jessie caught his passion. Now she matched it with her own, heaving her buttocks upward with a frenzy as furious as he expended in his violent, downward lunging.

Far sooner than she'd expected Jessie was taken by another shuddering, twisting climax. As it reached its peak, Tesunke yelled, a guttural cry from the depths of his chest. Then he drove with his own climactic lunge. He lay tense and shuddering for a long moment, then he sagged down on Jessie while her body was still quivering in her own declining spasm.

For a long moment neither of them spoke. At last Jessie said, "You are a very satisfying lover, Tesunke."

"And you are a fine companion on a blanket," he replied. "Even among the women of my own people I have not had such pleasure as you have brought me."

"I don't really want to move," Jessie sighed. "But—"

Tesunke broke in to say, "Do not move, then. We will rest a short while and enjoy another pleasant moment."

Jessie realized suddenly that unlike most of her lovers, Tesunke had not shriveled and faded after his climax. She could still feel his bulk filling her, and when she rolled her hips in a tentative questioning fashion he responded by thrusting, gently now, his moves as tentative as hers.

Tesunke's gentleness did not last long as Jessie continued her slow hip-rolls. Within a few moments the frenzy that had marked their first encounter returned, but now they took their pleasure slowly until the final few moments of their climax. Then Tesunke moved away and neither he nor Jessie spoke for several long moments as they lay together.

Jessie broke the silence. "We both need sleep," she said. "Tomorrow will be a long day, and the sun will be rising all too soon."

"You're right," he agreed. "We must get back as quickly as we can. But there will still be time to drive the cattle to the agency before the sun is up. Then we will bring my people together and when they have had food I will finish my teaching. There is still much to do, and perhaps I will find all the time I need now to do it."

★

Chapter 14

"All of us is real surprised about the way everything's happened, Miss Star," Matthew Green told Jessie. They were standing outside the Indian Agency buildings watching the stir of activity a short distance away.

"You're no more surprised than Ki and I are," Jessie assured the acting head of the agency. "But after your chief was killed, it looked like all of us were going to be in some really bad trouble."

"That's about how we felt, too, Miss Star," Green nodded. "Holed up down in that cellar the way we were, none of us had the least notion about what was going on. Then before poor old Rafe left to go see if you and your man would help us, he really laid down the law about meaning what he said. That was when he gave us strict orders not to poke our heads out until after the Indians had cooled down."

"Perhaps the Indians will settle down," Jessie went on, "Now that they have some good fresh meat instead of the rotten stuff they've been getting."

On the level turf beyond them the Indians were clustered in four large groups at the spots where the steers brought back by Jessie and Ki and Tesunke had been slaughtered. The men stood in rough circles around the steer carcasses, while the women worked at skinning the animals. Now and then one of the men stepped up to draw a sheath knife and trim off a small strip of meat, then started eating the raw flesh.

"I don't believe there'll be any question about them settling down," Ki remarked. "All they ever wanted was decent food."

"Which the rascals back East didn't send us, even when we asked," Green said. There was bitterness in his voice.

"I don't mind admitting that I was more than just upset when the Indians got word of Sitting Bull being killed," Jessie said. "And when they were attacking Ki and me in our cabin, things did look bad for a while."

"You and your friends sure saved our bacon," Green went on. "Getting here with them beeves just when you did. I never seen nobody as glad to get the meat from them steers as that bunch of redskins is."

"And they know the meat's fresh, not rotten," Ki put in.

"That makes a big difference," Green said. "Them scoundrels back East, they don't give a hoot about what we run into on the reservations. All they can think of is to set the army loose on the Indians when it looks like there's going to be trouble."

Jessie had been watching the Indians while Ki and Green were talking. She had looked vainly for Tesunke, unable to locate him in the flurry of activity around the area where the steers had been slaughtered. At last she saw him break away from a group of the Indian men and start toward the agency building.

"In just a minute or so we'll be able to find out how the Indians feel now," Jessie said. She gestured toward the group he was leaving. "Tesunke's coming over to join us, and he'll know what the Indians are planning to do."

Tesunke was within speaking distance of the trio now and close enough to them to hear Jessie's remark. He wasted no time in preliminaries when he stopped beside them, and said, "I think our troubles will soon be put behind us. Among our people the drums have been talking. The message that will interest you most is that the Sioux in the north of Dakota Territory have decided they will not follow the plan that the Indian Bureau had, to send them to Canada."

"Wait a minute!" Green broke in. "I never heard anything about the bureau planning something like that!"

"Some of your bureau people in the East made the plan," Tesunke told him. "Our northern tribes were told of it, but only a few liked it. The others did not want to go there."

"So they're staying on the reservation?" Jessie asked.

"Of course," Tesunke nodded. "But they will not stay on the land they have now. Many of our head chiefs, Long Toes and Standing Elk and Sitting Bull's people are traveling South, to join those who have found a peaceful place."

"With all the trouble they've been having, where will they find a place like that?" Ki frowned.

"It is a place I have seen myself," Tesunke replied. "And I will go to be with my people, many of them are there already."

"From what you say, it must be very nice," Jessie said.

"More than nice," Tesunke told her. "Our people will put up their tepees by a creek of sweet water in a green valley at the south of our reservation land."

"Does the valley have a name?" Jessie asked.

"Of course," Tesunke answered. "It takes its name from the creek. It is called Wounded Knee."

Watch for

**LONE STAR AND THE
HELLBOUND PILGRIMS**

113th novel in the exciting LONE STAR series
from Jove

Coming in January!

If you enjoyed this book, subscribe now and get...

TWO FREE

A $7.00 VALUE—